Tremarrow

TONY DWELLY

Tremarrow

The thrilling sequel to 'Julie's Meadow'

Romance and Remorse in an English Village

MEMOIRS

Cirencester

Published by Memoirs

MEMOIRS
PUBLISHING

25 Market Place, Cirencester, Gloucestershire, GL7 2NX
info@memoirsbooks.co.uk www.memoirspublishing.com

Copyright ©Tony Dwelly, July 2012

First published in England, July 2012

Book jacket design Ray Lipscombe

ISBN 978-1-909020-63-4

Printed in England

Chapter One

Things had settled down after the wedding at Tremarrow farm. The doctor had confirmed that both Julie and Sarah were pregnant. The lodge was full with visitors every week; this pleased George, Sarah's autistic brother and Jenny, the autistic girl from the convent, who had come to live with Fred and Julie. Both George and Jenny had wonderful personalities. All of the villagers loved both of them.

Breakfast had finished at the lodge, and Fred had taken all the visitors for a trip around the farm on the train that Cart the blacksmith had made. George had gone with them, but Jenny had stayed with Julie. She wanted to help her clear up the breakfast things. They were both so fond of each other. Julie suddenly started holding her stomach; Jenny could see she was in pain by the look on her face. "Are you feeling poorly?" Jenny asked.

"Oh, it will pass in a minute," Julie replied as she put the dishes in the sink. "Jenny, help me," she said, as she passed a couple of cups to Jenny.

Julie looked at her and smiled, but the pain in her stomach worsened.

"Look!" Jenny gasped, pointing to Julie's jeans. The front was covered in blood.

With one hand Julie touched the bloodspot and immediately realised what was happening. She was bent over double with pain. "Jenny dear, do you think you will be able to go up to the farm and fetch Sarah?"

"I'll go quickly," Jenny replied, hurrying out the door.

When Jenny got up to the farm, she was all flummoxed; she ran in to Sarah and started pulling at her arm. "Julie! Julie!" she shouted.

"Whatever is it?" Sarah asked, sensing something was wrong.

"Julie blood - Julie bleeding - Julie… poorly," Jenny said breathlessly. "Sarah, come quickly!" she added urgently.

John was out in the yard but came in to the kitchen, as he could hear Jenny shouting from outside.

"What is it?" he asked, as he entered the kitchen.

"It's Julie," Sarah said. "I have to go down to her. I think Jenny should stay here with you, and I think you should phone the doctor." She ran out the door.

When Sarah got down to the lodge, she found Julie on the floor in the lodge kitchen. She had undone her jeans - there was a lot of blood. "Oh my God, Julie; what is it?" she exclaimed.

The sweat was pouring off Julie's face. "I think I've had a miscarriage," she replied quite calmly.

"The doctor's on his way. Are you in much pain?" Sarah asked, not really knowing what to say or do.

It wasn't more than a few moments before the doctor arrived. He took one look at her and knew what was wrong. "You know what's happened, don't you?" he said, with a sad look on his face.

"Yes," Julie nodded.

"Is there a phone down here?" the doctor asked Sarah.

"Yes, it's in the house."

"I will phone for an ambulance; she will have to go to the hospital," the doctor said as he started writing on a pad.

"Does she need an ambulance? Can't we take her?" Sarah asked with concern.

"You could, I suppose, but you will have to drive gently. I will phone the hospital so that they will expect you."

Julie raised a slight smile as she looked at Sarah. "Don't you drive," she said.

"Why not? I'm a good driver," Sarah replied.

"Maybe, but I think I need someone with a licence to drive me."

Sarah laughed as she turned to the doctor. "How quickly do we have to get her there?" she asked.

"As quickly as possible, in case she haemorrhages," he replied.

"Will you stay with her a minute?" she asked the doctor. "I'll go and get John, and he can take her in; then I'll get Fred, and he can come in as soon as I get hold of him." Sarah was now talking methodically.

Sarah ran up to the farm to get John to go down with the car to take Julie to the hospital. "I wish I could go with her, but I will have to stay with Jenny and fetch Fred," she said, as John ran to his car.

"You should phone Cart and Olive; they will come over and look after the visitors and Jenny, and you could ride in with Fred," John said, as he closed the car door and sped down to the lodge. It wasn't long before he had Julie in hospital, where matron and a doctor where waiting.

By this time Jenny was getting very agitated. "I want Julie," she said. "My Julie."

"Come now," Sarah said, trying to calm her down. "We have to help Julie as she is feeling poorly; we will have to phone Cart to see if he can come and get Fred, so he can go and see Julie."

Sarah had hardly put the phone down when Cart and Olive came running in.

"How is she?" Olive asked anxiously.

"I don't know any more than I said on the phone," Sarah replied. "I need to get hold of Fred; he's gone around the farm with the train."

"I'll go get him," Cart said. "I'll take the tractor if that's all right."

"Off course it is," Sarah replied.

"What do you want me to do?" Olive asked enthusiastically.

"I would like to go to the hospital with Fred," Sarah said. "But there's Jenny to look after, and I don't know about the lodge. Someone will have to see to that because there will be lunches to do. Perhaps it would be better if I stayed and did that, and you go to the hospital with Fred." Sarah's voice was full of concern.

"Nonsense," Olive replied. "Julie will want you there, and besides, there is nothing I can't do down at the lodge." She looked at Jenny and put her arm around her. "Especially with this one's help," she said.

Jenny put on a little smile, but she was worried about Julie.

Olive looked at her. "Come on," she said. "We have to go and get everything ready for when Julie comes home; if we don't get it right, Julie will be cross."

"Julie is never cross," Jenny said quite angrily.

"I know; I was only teasing. Come on, let's go and get the lunches." Olive caught hold of Jenny's hand as they walked down to the lodge.

It wasn't long before Fred arrived with the train, with Cart right behind on the tractor. Fred's feet never touched the ground as he ran over to his car and drove up to pick Sarah up. She was walking down towards the lodge. The car had hardly stopped when Sarah jumped in and they made their way to Tavistock Hospital at great speed. When they got there, they were met by John, who was out in the courtyard not knowing what to do or say.

"How is she?" Fred shouted as they approached John.

"I don't know, they won't tell me anything," John said as they all entered the hospital through the main door. "They are waiting for you; she's in the second door down the corridor."

"Do you want me to wait here?" Sarah asked as Fred made for the corridor.

"I'd like you to come," he replied, as he pushed open the door to the corridor where he was met by Matron.

"Can I help you?" Matron asked in a rather stern voice.

Fred explained who they were, and then Matron turned and took them down to the ward where Julie was. It was a small ward with just four beds. Julie was in the bed by the window. She saw them enter and raised a little smile.

Fred went to her quickly and kissed her gently on the forehead. He didn't say a word as tears ran down his face.

Matron left them and went back to the waiting room where John was sitting. "Tell me," she said, "you all live on a farm, don't you?" She came and sat down beside John.

"Yes," he replied.

"Do you have any sheep lambing that Julie could have come in contact with?" Matron asked with concern.

"Why yes; we have some down at the lodge for the visitors to see."

"Don't you know that pregnant woman should not go near sheep, especially if they are lambing? Have you ever heard of chamydiosis, or toxoplasmosis and Q-fever?"

"Yes," John replied. "They are ailments that sheep get, but they aren't serious."

"Not to sheep," Matron said. "Although they aren't that common, if someone who is pregnant gets any of them, they nearly always abort, and I would say that is what has happened in this case." She tapped John on the knee as she stood up.

"My God, it's my fault!" he said, as he dropped his head into his hands.

"Don't be too hard on yourself. Like I said, it is very rare now, and people don't think about it like they used to." Matron made her way towards the door.

John got up and made his way quickly to the ward where Julie was. He opened the door and went in. "However can you forgive me?" he asked, as he went over to Julie.

"What is it?" Sarah asked. She was standing at the end of the bed.

"It's the sheep; pregnant women should not go near sheep! They can catch something that makes them abort," John said. "I should have known that; it's my fault; I should have known."

"Don't be silly," Julie replied. "It's no one's fault; last night one of the newborn lambs got through the fence. I picked it up and put it back with its mother. Do you think that's what did it?"

"Most certainly," came a voice by the doorway. It was Matron. She had come to tell them to leave now and let Julie have some rest. They said their goodbyes and left. Fred told her he would be back that night.

"Not until seven o'clock," Matron insisted.

John and Sarah drove back, and Fred drove back on his own. As soon as they got back to the lodge, John rushed down to Fred. He needed to talk to him because he was feeling so guilty about the sheep. He could not stop apologizing.

"You weren't to know," Fred said, as he led John over to the gate that led from the yard into the field. "I am so upset and disappointed with what's happened, but would you deprive these people of this?" he said, pointing to the sheep in the field. Cart and the autistic children were playing with the sheep and lambs. "Yes, had we known what was going to happen, we would have kept Julie well away from them, but please don't blame yourself. I should have known as well."

"I don't know if I can accept it like you have," John said, as he rested his hand on Fred's shoulder.

"Trust me. I keep asking questions like 'Why us?', 'Why Julie?' - she would be such a good mother."

They were both leaning on the gate. Cart hadn't noticed them. Olive came over from clearing up after the lunches. "How is the poor girl?" she asked with a tone of concern.

"You know, Julie's not showing her feelings; she's just worrying about the visitors," Fred said. He had a quiver in his voice as he said it.

"You tell her not to worry, Cart, and I have everything under control. We have made up the spare bed in the lodge and we will sleep here tonight." Olive put her arm around Fred and gave him a hug.

"You are all so kind," Fred said. Suddenly, he looked and saw Sarah walking down towards them. "Go back!" he shouted. "Don't come near the sheep."

"Oh, I never thought - " she shouted back. "I just want to know if there is anything I can do?"

"Everything is all under control," Olive said, walking over towards her.

It wasn't long before Andrew the vicar arrived, asking about Julie. He was followed by half the village; the news had spread through the village like wildfire.

Jenny and George were in the field with Cart and the visitors. Jenny came running over as soon as she noticed Fred. "Julie," she said. "Where's Julie?" She was getting quite agitated.

"Julie's fine," Olive said, trying to reassure Jenny. "Fred's going in to see her presently. She will be home tomorrow, and Cart and I will look after you tonight.

"I go with Fred," Jenny replied. "I go."

"Oh, I don't think they will let you in the hospital," Olive said as she smiled at her. "You will see Julie tomorrow when she comes home. Besides, I need you to show me and Cart what we have to do."

"Jenny show you; then Jenny go with Fred," she replied.

"I think we should let her come with me; if she sees Julie, she will probably settle then," Fred said.

"You better take Sarah with you just in case she can't go in or gets upset," John suggested.

It wasn't long before they had all had their tea, and John, Sarah and Jenny made their way to the hospital. When they got there, Matron said Julie had slept all afternoon and was quite chirpy, considering, so all three of them could see her just for a while.

As they entered the ward, the excitement on Jenny's face cheered every one up; she ran over to the bed. "My Julie," she said, with a large smile.

Julie was pleased to see her; she put her hand out for her to catch hold.

Jenny sat on the chair beside the bed, catching hold of Julie's hand. Fred leaned over from the bottom of the bed and gave Julie a kiss. There wasn't room for him to get beside the bed, so he and Sarah sat on a chair at the bottom of the bed.

Jenny squeezed Julie's hand. "Aunty Julie," she said. "George said you haven't got a baby in your tummy anymore."

"No darling, I'm afraid not," Julie replied with a sob.

"Aunty Julie, does that mean you won't be a mummy?"

"Not just at the moment, but you never know what might happen in the future."

"Aunty Julie?" Jenny paused.

"What is it dear?" Julie asked.

"Well, if you aren't having a baby, will you be my Mummy?"

Julie had tears flowing down her cheeks, and so did Fred and Sarah. "Would you like that?" Julie asked, as she had a little sniffle.

"Yes, I've never had a mummy before. I would like that very much."

"I think I would like it too," Julie replied as she dried her eyes on the end of the sheet.

Sarah dried her eyes. "I think we should go outside for a minute and let Fred and Julie have a few minutes alone," she said to Jenny, as she winked her eye at Julie.

Sarah and Jenny went out into the waiting room and sat down. It wasn't long before they were joined by Matron. Jenny sat on a chair and swung her legs back and forward. "I've got a mummy now," she said to Matron.

"Have you dear? That's good," Matron replied with a large smile.

<h1 style="text-align:center">Chapter Two</h1>

It was a couple of days before Julie came home from hospital. The first day was quite tiring for her, as most of the village paid her a visit, and Jenny never left her side. Poor George spent most of the day sitting outside on the steps waiting for Jenny to come out. Julie told Jenny on a number of occasions to ask him to come in but to no avail.

That evening just before tea, Julie said, "I must go out and get some fresh air." She looked at Jenny. "Are you and George going to walk up to Sarah's with me?"

"Yes Mummy," she replied.

As they walked down the steps from the cottage, Jenny said, "Mummy, you know Auntie Sarah has a robin. She says it is her baby. Will your baby be a bird?"

"Oh, I don't know dear. My baby hadn't turned in to a proper baby, but I would like to think so," Julie said with a tear in her eye.

"Look!" George said, as they walked across the lodge yard. Sitting in the middle of the gate and singing its heart out was a robin. It had its bright red chest fluffed up and it sounded like it was singing, "Here I am!"

"It's your baby," Jenny said. "It could be my brother."

Julie's face lit up with a little joy, but her eyes just filled with tears.

When they got up to the farm, Jenny ran on in and told Sarah what they had seen.

Julie stayed up at the farm, chatting away with Sarah before she and Jenny made their way back home. George had stayed up at the farm. With every step they made, they could hear "cheep, cheep, cheep". Sometimes they could see the robin on a branch, and sometimes he was hiding in a tree, but he was with them all the way home.

The next morning, Julie told Jenny that it wasn't fair to George that she was spending so much time with her.

"But I have to look after you," she replied.

"Well, I'm better now thanks to your nursing, and today I have things to do. So you and George can help Fred with the visitors."

"If you're sure - I think you are the best Mummy ever," Jenny said, as she put her arms around Julie and hugged her.

Julie wanted some time to herself, as Fred was fussing over her, coming in every five minutes to see if she was all right. He wasn't doing much with the visitors, as he didn't want to be too far away from Julie. "I'm going for a walk on my own today," she told him. "So you must take the visitors out today."

Fred agreed, but he didn't want to take them too far. He had hired a bus for the next day because it was Widacomb Fair day, and he was taking them all there.

Julie had forgotten all about that. "Will you be able to manage without me?" she asked Fred with concern. "I don't know if I will feel quite up to it."

"That's fine. Cart and Olive have both said they will

come. I'm more concerned about leaving you," Fred said, as he put his arms around her.

It wasn't long before Fred had boarded all the visitors and George and Jenny on the train for a trip around the farm.

It was a beautiful day, and Julie had decided she was going for a walk up to the meadow. She hadn't been there since the loss of her baby; she hardly missed a day before that. It was a place she went to pray; it was her church and her heaven. She slowly walked through the flowers and got to the edge of the pond. She sat down and her face lit up with a smile as she remembered what had gone on there-the first time she and Fred made love, the time they were both naked in the grass, and the remembrance they held for Sarah's little girl. Julie remembered the harvest festival when she had a drop too much of Gilbert Lanes cider, and of course her wedding, which was the most beautiful day of her life.

Julie sat there for a couple of hours, one minute crying, and the next laughing to herself, when suddenly she was startled by a man's voice. "I thought I might find you here," it said softly.

Julie turned around startled. It was Andrew, the vicar.

"You made me jump," she said, as she stood up from the grass to greet him.

"How are you?" he asked. "We all worry about you."

"Oh, I'm doing fine," she replied. "I have times when I think, 'Why me?' I have times when I blame God; I have times when I blame myself, but deep down I know it's just one of those things that happen, and on the whole I'm one lucky girl to have the things and people I love around me all the time."

"You certainly are someone very special," Andrew replied, as they started to walk together towards the gate.

"Me, special?" Julie replied with a laugh. "You wouldn't think so if you saw me nagging Fred sometimes."

Andrew laughed. "You will always be special to me and to the people who know you."

"I'm going into Sarah's for a cup of tea," Julie said as they neared the farm. "Are you coming?"

"Do you think she will mind?"

"Of course not - we are special people, remember? We are welcome anywhere."

Andrew laughed as they walked across the yard, where they were met by Sarah.

"By the look of the smiles on your two faces," Sarah said, "I would think you had been up to no good if I didn't know you better."

Andrew went bright red. "Oh, how could you say such a thing," he replied, like a bashful child.

They went indoors where they were joined by John. They all sat around the kitchen table. Andrew said he was going to call in and see Jan Symons on the way back, as his wife was quite worried about him.

"What's wrong?" John asked. "I haven't seen him down with his horse lately; I know Fred's been looking in to make sure the horse is all right. His wife thinks he is pining away. He misses the farm so much that he just can't accept that it's gone. I was hoping my plans for retired animals would have taken off, but I think that was just pie in the sky. I thought that would have given him plenty to do."

John looked deep in thought as he kept talking.

"It's a pity, because something like that would have helped. I know he looks old, but it was all to do with the financial worry he had on the farm. He isn't sixty-five until sometime next year."

Jan had to give up his small farm up on the moor, as he found it difficult to make ends meet. He knew if he didn't sell up when he did, he would be thrown out with nothing, and that wouldn't have been fair to his wife. So he sold up and moved into a cottage, which had been left to Olive by Lord Trelivan, as she had moved in with Cart. Jan had kept his horse, Jess, which ran free down in the fields by the lodge.

John thought for a minute. He looked at Andrew excitedly. "Can you get Jan down to the pub tonight? I have an idea."

"I don't know; it might be a bit of a job," Andrew replied. "He doesn't move from his chair - you might have to go around and see him."

"No, I don't think that will work. I don't think he should think we are doing him any favours," John said, beaming all over his face.

"What is it?" Sarah asked. "How can we help him?"

"If Andrew can get him there, you will all see then," John said with a smile.

"You could tell him Fred wants to know all about Widecombe Fair, as he is taking the visitors there tomorrow," Julie said. She was as anxious as the rest to know what the plan was.

Andrew got up and started to leave. "I'll get him there for seven, even if I have to drag him," he said with a smile.

"Are you going tonight?" Sarah asked Julie as she was leaving.

"You bet - I have to know what John's little secret is," Julie replied as she walked out the door. John walked out to the yard close behind her. Julie turned towards him. "You are such a kind man," she said.

"How can you say that" - he replied - "after I killed your baby?"

"You didn't kill my baby; it was a freak of nature that killed my baby," Julie replied quite sternly.

"I know you say that because you're so forgiving, but I know it was my fault. I should never have put those sheep down there; it will live with me forever."

John started to cry and Julie put her arms around him. "Now listen to me," she said firmly, "I don't blame you, and Fred doesn't blame you. No one thinks it's your fault."

Sarah looked out the door and saw John in Julie's arms and came running over. "What is it?" she shouted. "What the hell is going on?"

Julie broke away from John. "You want to talk some sense into this husband of yours. He has some stupid notion that he is responsible for the loss of my baby."

"I have told him and told him," Sarah replied. "He gets up in the night and walks around. I just don't know how to convince him."

"I think people have spent too much time worrying about me and not thinking about John," Julie said.

"It was the way Matron said it," John replied. "I should have known, and once she said it, I remembered. But it was too late then; it makes me an irresponsible farmer." He rubbed his hand over his head.

"It's my farm as well," Sarah said, "so if you are irresponsible, then so am I."

"You didn't put the sheep down there, I did," John said angrily.

"Stop it, the pair of you!" Julie shouted. She burst into tears. "Why don't you understand that I don't want it to be anyone's fault; it hasn't got to be anyone's fault. It happened, and that's all there is to it. I just want help to get over it, and people trying to blame themselves won't help."

Julie was sobbing loudly. Both John and Sarah put their arms around her. "Not another mention," Sarah said firmly.

"And what about you, John?" Julie asked as they broke away.

"Not a mention, I promise," he said with a smile.

"That's good," Julie replied. "Fred and I will see you at a quarter to seven tonight. I think the pub might do me some good." She hastily made her way back to the lodge.

That evening, Jenny and George stayed in the lodge with the visitors so that Fred and Julie could go out; they met John and Sarah at a quarter to seven and made their way to the pub. Much of the talk at the pub was about Widacombe Fair. Gilbert Lane said he no longer goes there because of what had happened there three years in a row.

"What was that?" Julie asked.

"'Twas the hairy hands," Gilbert replied.

"What hairy hands?" Sarah asked, laughing.

"The one's that caught hold of the steering wheel on the way home."

"What nonsense," Olive said bluntly.

"'Tis true I tell ye," Gilbert said. "The first time Billy Coad came through Post Bridge coming home - " Gilbert was talking in an almost ghostly voice. He had the girls mesmerised, with their mouths wide open. "As he got to the straight bit of road, a pair of hairy hands caught hold of the steering wheel and steered it off the road."

"Gosh," Julie said.

Gilbert continued, "And then the next year, the same thing happened to Sam Masters, and the third year, bugger me, if in the same spot, the same thing didn't happen to George Blight. It frightened me. I was so lucky I was in my van behind him when he left the road."

"Gosh, what do you think, Olive? Is there such a thing?" Sarah asked. She had believed every word.

"Ask him how much cider they drank that day. I think you will find that's where the answer lies."

"What do you think, Cart?" Julie asked.

"I'm with Olive. I think it was all down to the cider."

No one had noticed that Andrew and Jan Symons had come into the pub until they heard Jan's voice bellow out, "'Tis true, and it shouldn't be taken lightly!"

"What's true?" Fred asked, with a laugh. "The cider or the hairy hands?" Everyone had a little giggle.

"You can laugh," Jan said calmly. "Knowing Gilbert's friends, I bet cider played its part, but you shouldn't take the hands lightly. People have lost their lives to the hands. Sheep have been killed, single girls have become pregnant, and hairy babies have been born."

"Gosh, have you ever seen them?" Sarah asked.

"Once many years ago, I bought some pigs from old Tommy Burns," Jan began. "He lived over near Post Bridge. I hitched up the cart to Jess, and we went and picked up the pigs. Coming back, it started to rain heavily; we just got to the spot that Gilbert talked about - when suddenly something pulled hard on the reins. I struggled and struggled, but the horse was heading right for the moor. The pigs in the back were squealing, and I could see the hairy hands in front of mine on the reins." Jan paused.

"What happened?" Julie asked. "How did you get out of it?"

"There was a large flash of lightning, and the largest clap of thunder I have ever heard - and the hands just let go and vanished."

"Do you believe it now, Olive?" Sarah asked.

"Let's just say I'm still sceptical," she replied.

John, Sarah, Fred, Julie, Cart and Olive went and sat around the large table in the corner of the pub. "Come and join us," John shouted to Andrew and Jan, as he was waiting to put his idea forward. They came and joined them.

John thought he should address Cart to avoid making it look like he was trying to help Jan. "Cart," he said cheerfully, "you don't know anyone that wants a job without much pay, do you?"

Cart laughed. "I don't think there is anyone who doesn't want a lot of pay. Why do you ask?"

"Well," he said, "farming is changing; there's a company over Callington way that is building chicken houses that hold twenty thousand chickens. I was in the market last week, and I was told of someone that had over a thousand sows all kept indoors; if we don't watch it, our children will lose farming as we know it, forever."

"So what can you do?" Cart asked. "You can't stop progress."

"I might not be able to stop progress, nor would I want to, but I would love to preserve a bit of the past."

"And how do you think you could do that?" Andrew asked, a large frown on his face.

"Well, if I could find someone to run it, I would turn the twenty-five acres down by the church into a mini-farm with a few sows and free-range chickens. It's not big enough to keep much else, but there are buildings there, and I think it's just the place."

"It's surprising what you can do with twenty-five acres," Jan said. "I only had thirty."

"There you go then," John said. "All I need is the right man."

"I could do it if you like," Jan said quite shyly.

"Oh, I couldn't expect you to do it; after all, you have only just retired," John replied, trying hard to hide his excitement that he had done what he had set out to do.

"I don't enjoy retirement much," Jan said quietly, "so I would rather like to give it a go." Jan hoped John would say yes.

"Well, on one condition; you will be doing me a big favour,

and if you want to stop, you tell me." John held his hand out for Jan to shake.

Every one raised their glasses to the new venture.

Chapter Three

The next morning, the visitors and half the village had gone to Widecomb Fair. Julie had gone up to the meadow to pick some flowers to put on Sarah's baby's grave. When she went in to the graveyard and walked towards the grave, she noticed a little girl of about four or five sitting on the bench under an old beech tree. She was swinging her legs back and forward. As Julie put the flowers on the grave, she kept an eye on the little girl, who she hadn't seen before.

Julie spent a few moments arranging the flowers and saying a little prayer. She was just about to leave when the little girl came over to her. "Hello," a little voice said.

"Oh hello," Julie replied. "And what's your name?"

"I'm Amy," the little girl replied. "What's your name?"

"I'm Julie, I haven't seen you before. Are you visiting someone?"

"We have just moved in down there," the little girl said, pointing to the cottage beside the church.

"That's nice. I might see you some more; I live next to my friends' farm, and you will be able to come over and see the animals."

"I don't expect so. We are on the run, and I shouldn't talk to anyone," Amy said in a whisper.

"How do you mean, on the run?"

"We moved here when it was dark; a man who Mummy knew brought us," Amy replied quite excitedly.

"I see. Perhaps I shouldn't ask any more questions then." Julie was feeling a little nervous.

Suddenly, a woman of about thirtyish appeared. "Amy!" she shouted. "Come here."

The woman was dressed in a short black skirt - certainly the shortest Julie had ever seen. She had high heels that she could hardly walk in.

"I have to go," Amy said and ran back towards the women.

"Hello!" Julie shouted to the women. But she did not reply; she just hurried back to the cottage by the church.

Julie made her way back to Sarah's, wondering what she should do and who they were on the run from. Was it the police? She told Sarah all about it and anxiously asked her what they should do about it.

"Nothing," Sarah replied. "If they have done something wrong, and there is a little girl there, they will soon be found."

"You're probably right, but I do worry about the little girl," Julie said. "The woman sounded quite fierce."

"Why don't you go and see Andrew," Sarah suggested. "He must know something. After all, the cottage belongs to the church."

"That's a good idea. Why didn't I think of that? I'll go over there now," Julie said, making for the door.

"I think you should have a cup of coffee first," Sarah said, as she put the kettle switch down.

"Make it a quick one then," Julie replied. She pulled out a chair from under the kitchen table and sat down.

As they were drinking their coffee, a car drove into the yard. Sarah got up and went to the door. It was Mr Knight, the solicitor. "Fancy seeing you," Sarah said, as she showed him into the kitchen.

"Good morning to you both," he said.

"Have you come about the woman in the church cottage?" Julie asked, full of excitement.

"I'm afraid I don't know any woman in any cottage," he replied.

"Let's hope it's just a social visit then," Sarah said. "It's been a long time since you came around."

"It's not a social visit either," he said. He opened his briefcase and took out a newspaper. "This is tomorrow's local paper," he said. "Now do either of you know a Lenard James?"

"The name rings a bell," Sarah said.

"You should remember him," Julie said. "He's a couple of years older than us. He lived up near Princetown somewhere. You must remember, Sarah - he had a big crush on you at school." Julie smiled.

"I think I would have remembered that, but why do you ask?" Sarah replied.

"The editor phoned me and asked me to come and get a copy of the paper before it goes out," Mr Knight said.

He spread out the paper. The headlines read: "Juror Knew Trelivan Was Guilty Before the Trial." It went on to say that a former boyfriend of Sarah Brite, the daughter of murder victim Molly Page, sat on the jury that convicted

Rupert Trelivan of Page's murder. The newspaper was alerted by local man Brian Furze. He said he thought a great injustice had been done and was looking to the paper to put it right. On receiving this information, the paper informed the local police, and as they went to press, James was helping them with their inquiries.

"I don't understand," Sarah said. "He has never been my boyfriend. I only ever went out with John. How can they say these things?"

"What does it mean?" Julie asked.

"It means whether he was an old boyfriend or not, he must have known Rupert, and he should have said so at the trial. Then he would have been dismissed."

"We all know Brian Furze; he's a right shark," Sarah said. "He was a mate of Rupert's; he'd help himself to anything that wasn't nailed down; I bet there's money behind this."

"It won't make any difference to Rupert though, will it?" Julie asked.

"I'm afraid it makes a big difference; I am not sure what, as I haven't ever come across it before, and I haven't had a chance to do any research, but I think you should prepare yourself. He could be set free," Mr Knight said as he picked up his cup and drank the last drop of tea.

"How could he be set free? It was a unanimous decision, so he is only one out of twelve," Sarah said quite angrily.

"It's not quite like that; the first thing his lawyers will say is he would have influenced the other members of the jury."

"I don't understand; everyone knows he is guilty, so surely that's all there is too it," Julie said quite emphatically.

"Seriously, what do you think will happen? Will he be retried" Sarah asked.

"I honestly don't know. I will have to speak to the barristers. I have never heard of anything like it before; it will probably go to high court for the lords to make a decision. To answer your question - if the court decides he has to be set free and they decide it counts as a not guilty verdict, then he can't be recharged. But they might find some other answer. I just don't know. I expect the police will want to ask you a few questions," Mr Knight said as he caught hold of Sarah's hand and patted her wrist with the other hand.

"Well, we will just have to wait and see," Sarah replied. "Thanks for coming over and letting us know."

"I must get on now. I will go to the police station on the way and find out if they want to speak to you. If they do, and you want me present, I will make an appointment. Now I will bid you good day and phone you in the morning."

As Mr Knight was leaving, Julie said, "Well, what do you think of that? It could only happen to that bugger."

"I don't know what to think," Sarah said. "I'm not going to worry about it. I have my bump to worry about, and nothing is going to happen to this one." She placed her hand on the bottom of her tummy.

Julie came over and put her arms around her. Julie had a tear in her eye as she said, "I won't let anyone hurt your bump."

Sarah saw she was hiding her tears. "I'm so sorry," she said. "How insensitive of me - I didn't think about yours."

"Oh don't worry," Julie said, drying her eyes. "Of course I'm sad about it; you know I don't always agree with Andrew, but he always say's that God works in mysterious ways, and I think he is possibly right. If I hadn't had a miscarriage, then Jenny would never have asked me to be her mother. The smile on her face just overfills me with joy every time she comes in, so I can't be all sad."

"Julie, you are a remarkable person," Sarah said. "I'm so lucky to have you for a friend." She leaned forward and kissed her on the cheek.

"I've got to go," Julie said. "I want to see Andrew to see if he knows who is in the cottage."

Julie made her way down to the church. She couldn't find Andrew in the vicarage, so she went around to the church. The door was open; she could hear voices. She thought it rude to go in, so she sat on the seat in the graveyard.

Andrew had entered the church just before Julie. Sitting on the front pew was the woman from the cottage. She still was dressed in the shortest black skirt. The tops of her legs were showing above her stockings. Her legs were slightly apart, showing her black knickers. Her boobs were almost dropping out of the top of her blouse.

Andrew walked down and stood in front of her. "Are you all right my dear?" he asked, not knowing where to look.

"Tell me," she said. "Is there really a God?"

"I do hope so; my job's gone for a burden if there isn't," Andrew replied.

"Then why hasn't he helped me, am I that bad a person?"

"I don't think anyone is so bad in God's eyes that they don't deserve some help."

"Do you know - this is the first time I have been inside a church?"

"I hope it won't be the last," Andrew smiled. "I hope whatever your troubles are, you can find some comfort in here."

"It's so peaceful and cold, yet warming," the woman said. She looked up at Andrew and smiled. She had the most beautiful face.

"If you want to talk at any time, my door is always open," he said. "I don't want to pry into your troubles, but if you want someone to talk to, I'm a good listener - or if you would sooner talk to a lady, I might know someone who would help."

"The last thing I want right now is a busy body," she said. She got up and ran out of the church, crying as she stopped in the doorway to dry her eyes. She saw Julie sitting on the bench, looking at her. "What are you looking at, you nosy bitch?" she shouted, as she ran into the cottage.

Julie went into the church. Andrew was up at the altar praying. She went quietly up to the front pew and sat down. Andrew turned to see her.

"Hello my dear," he said and sat down beside her.

"I didn't interrupt you, did I?" Julie asked.

"No, my dear; it's nice to see you here. How are things?"

"Lots going on," she replied. She then told Andrew all about Mr Knight's visit to Sarah.

"How is Sarah taking it?"

"Very well I think; she seems she isn't going to let anything get to her that might affect her baby."

"Good for her - no need to worry until we know what's

going to happen. It's best left to the experts to sort out."

"Who's your new friend I saw leavening in a hurry?" Julie asked, in a sarcastic tone.

"I don't know who she is or were she comes from," Andrew replied.

"She's in a church cottage, and you don't know who she is? Bit strange someone like that in a church cottage, don't you think?" Julie said.

"Like what."

"Well, you know, like that?" Julie said, putting the emphases on the *like that*.

"I found her quite charming in a funny sort of way," Andrew replied.

"You wouldn't have found her charming if you knew what she called me," Sarah said firmly.

"Oh, and what was that?"

"Nosey bitch," Julie whispered.

"Oh, bitch wasn't very nice, was it now," Andrew said with a laugh.

Julie looked at him and smiled. "What about the nosey?" she asked.

"What about it?" Andrew asked with a big grin.

"Do you think I'm nosey?" Julie looked at Andrew in a sad way.

"Of course not my dear; I'm only teasing. Now about our new friend, I truly don't know where she comes from. I had a phone call from the bishop asking me if the cottage was still empty. He said someone would be arriving in the middle of the night, and she wanted her identity kept secret, and that's all I know. There's a very troubled soul inside that body."

"If you haven't seen the soul, you have seen most of the body," Julie said with a laugh. She looked at Andrew. "Why, I do believe you are blushing!" she said.

"Nonsense," he replied abruptly. "I think we will gradually get to know her and her daughter, and I'm sure there is something special there somewhere."

"You're such a sweetie, Andrew," Julie said. "Now I have to go; they will all be back soon from Widacombe."

"I hope they haven't seen the hairy hands," he said with a laugh as Julie left.

As Julie made her way back, the bus pulled up beside her. You could hear everyone on the bus singing above the noise of the engine. Jenny was the first off. She was just full of excitement. "Mummy-Mummy!" she shouted. "Me and George had six goes on the hobby horse."

"Did you darling? I'm glad you enjoyed it," Julie said, putting her arm around her as they walked down to the lodge.

Chapter Four

It was a couple of days before the police came and questioned Sarah. Julie came up to the farm along with Mr Knight to be with John and Sarah when the police arrived. The police inspector asked how well they knew Lenard James.

"I know of him," Sarah said. "He is quite a bit older than me, but we were at Tavistock School at the same time. But to say he was an old boyfriend - that's totally untrue."

"I know. In all fairness, James told us that was untrue; it seems something that Brian Furze added to the story along with many other points," the inspector said. "What about you, John? How well do you know Lenard James?" The inspector picked up the cup of coffee that Julie had put in front of him.

"Much the same as Sarah, really. I have seen him around the market a few times just to pass the time of day, and that's about it."

"Could you tell us what Mr James has said to you?" Mr Knight asked.

"Not a lot really - much the same as you pair really. I think he was quite embarrassed by the girlfriend thing. He made a stupid mistake. He was in the pub and had too much to drink - the topic of Lord Trelivan came up, and he said he was on the jury. Foolishly, he said he knew what a brute Rupert was before the trial, and of course Brian Furze was in the pub, and that's how it all got out."

"What happens now?" John asked the inspector.

"I will put my report in to the prosecution service. Whether they will take action against Lenard James - I don't know. But I think they will want to charge him with perjury. As for how it affects Rupert, that's up to his legal team to fight."

"Let's hope people will see sense and realise that there could have been only one verdict, and they will just brush it all to the side," Julie said as she picked up the empty cups from the table.

"If only you made the rules," Mr Knight said. "But I'm afraid life is not like that."

"How long do you think it will take before a decision is made?" John asked.

"I will probably be charging Mr James tomorrow, but it will be months before a decision is made on Rupert - there will be all sorts of legal battles."

The inspector started to walk towards the door, but then paused. "Be prepared to get some attention from the national press; I have heard from a good source that one of the big Sunday papers is going to run it as their main story."

"I hope not. I don't think I could face that," Sarah said, as she walked over to the door behind the inspector.

"You will be all right," Julie said. "We won't let them get to you, and besides, you have done nothing wrong, so you have nothing to worry about."

The inspector and Mr Knight both left, reassuring Sarah that they would both do their best to keep Rupert in jail.

After they had left, Julie asked Sarah if she wanted to go for a walk. She thought it might do her good.

"I don't know; I feel like I could do with a lie down. All this commotion has made me feel quite weak," Sarah replied as she sat down in the armchair.

"That's probably best," John said. "Do you want me to stay? I was going to get a load of straw and take it over to Jan for the pigs."

"No, you go on. I'm just going to lie down for a while. I'll be all right then. That goes for you too, Julie," Sarah said as she looked at her across the room.

"Are you sure?" Julie said. "I will come up later and see how you are."

Julie left and walked out across the yard.

As she turned down to the lodge, she was met by Amy, the little girl. "Hello - I have been down there," she said, pointing down towards the lodge.

"Did you see anyone?" Julie asked her.

Amy screwed her face up. "Funny people," she replied with a smile. "They made me frightened."

Julie lifted her up on to the wall. Then she sat on the wall beside her. "They are nice people," she said. "They just haven't been as lucky as us; they just take a bit longer to grow up than me and you."

"I'm a big girl," Amy replied. "Mummy said so, because I kept very quiet when she got me out of bed to come here."

"That's good. I would like to meet your mummy. Do you think she will meet me?"

"She said we must talk to no one - no matter what," Amy said, waving her finger as she spoke.

"I think I should take you home. Mummy might be worried about you." Julie jumped down off the wall and lifted Amy down.

They walked down the road and got to the cottage. The door was open and the woman was standing in the porch. She first saw Amy. "I just thought I might have to go and look for you; you know you shouldn't go out," she said crossly.

"She has been all right," Julie said. "I brought her back as soon as I saw her."

"Oh, it's you," the woman said, eying Julie up and down.

"That's right - the nosey bitch," she replied with a smile.

"Oh, I'm sorry about that. I didn't mean anything by it," the woman replied. She too managed a smile.

"I'm Julie, by the way," she said, holding out her hand.

"I know. The old vicar told me."

"I don't think Andrew would appreciate the *old* bit," Julie said, still smiling and hoping she had broken the ice.

"I'm Angie," the woman said, taking Julie's hand and shaking it. "But I keep myself to myself, mind."

"That's fine - but just remember, if you want anything, don't be afraid to ask, or if you want someone to look after Amy, I'm not far away."

"Thank you," she replied. Julie started to walk down the path when Angie shouted to her. Julie turned and walked back. "There is something I would like."

"What's that?" Julie asked, sounding astonished that she had called her back.

"I don't really know how to ask; it's embarrassing."

"Try me, I can only say no," Julie said, trying to reassure her.

"Well, have you got any clothes you could let me have? All I got is what I got on. I managed to pack Amy's clothes, but none of mine. I only have one pair of knickers - I will pay you."

"I will go shopping in Tavistock with you if you like," Julie said. "After all, you wouldn't want to where my knickers," Julie said laughing.

"No, I can't go out. I might be seen. I can't risk that," Angie said in a quite definite way.

"That's fine," Julie said. "I will see what I can do. I know I have some new pants at home, and I am sure I could find a dress or two; it might not be what you are used to, mind."

"Thank God for that," Angie replied with a smile, as Julie ran off down the path.

Julie thought she had better call in and make sure Sarah was all right. She opened the door, and Sarah was sitting in the armchair in the kitchen. "Are you all right?" she asked, quite startled to see her there.

"I'm fine. I tried a lie down, but couldn't stay there."

Julie told Sarah all about Angie and the clothes. "I think I misjudged her; she seems quite nice - very frightened about something though."

"Let's go and turn my wardrobe inside out, and see what we can find. I can't wear any of it now," Sarah said excitedly.

The pair of them were more excited about going through Sarah's clothes than they would have been going shopping. They spent most of the day rummaging through Sarah's things, holding them up to each other and twirling around. They packed some dresses, blouses and a couple of pairs of jeans in a flat box after Sarah insisted they should be ironed. While Sarah was ironing, Julie nipped down to the lodge and picked up a pack of pants and a couple of pairs of shoes, one with a slight hill and a black flat pair. She got back to the farm just as Sarah had put the last blouse neatly in the box.

"There you go," Sarah said. "Let's hope it's for a good cause."

"I think she will appreciate it. I can't imagine her in them though," Julie said, picking up the box.

"You better not tell her they're mine; she might not like to think you have told anyone," Sarah said, as Julie went out the door.

Julie took the clothes over to Angie, who asked her in. "I don't know if they're any good to you; they might not fit," she said as she placed the box on the table.

"They're perfect. I'm sure they will; I like going in the church, but I haven't been in there today in case the vicar was there," Angie said, picking up one of the dresses and holding it up against her torso.

"You don't want to worry about Andrew; I wouldn't stay away because of him. He would be pleased to see you."

"It's not that; he might see more than he bargained for - I got no knickers on," Angie said with a laugh.

Julie laughed with her. "Look, I have to go," she said. "Keep it up; it's lovely to see you smile."

"Let me pay you," Angie said, as Julie got to the door.

"You already have," she replied.

"How?"

"By looking so happy. I just hope it goes a little way to helping you over your troubles." Julie said bye to Amy and left.

After Julie had gone, Angie tried on the clothes, with Amy sitting on a stool and clapping every time she came out wearing something different. The last thing she tried on was a pink, sateen-looking dress. It was only slightly low cut and finished just above the knee. She looked absolutely stunning. One would have thought she was someone out of a Cliff Richard rock-and-roll film; she twirled round and round with the dress floating out.

"You are beautiful Mummy," Amy said.

Angie looked at herself in the mirror. She had tears rolling down her cheeks as she went over and picked Amy up and danced around with her in her arms. Then she put Amy down. "Just sit here a minute. I will only be a little while; I'm just going to the church to say a little prayer."

As she entered the church, Andrew was standing by the altar. He turned as the clonk of the latch on the large oak door alerted him to someone coming in. His jaw dropped when he saw her standing in the doorway, with the sun shining in behind her. "Beautiful," he whispered.

"What do you think?" she asked, as she did a little twirl in the doorway.

"Very nice," Andrew replied, with a smile that lit up the whole church.

"I can't stay. Amy is on her own, but I was so excited with the clothes, I thought I must say a little prayer."

"I will say one with you if you like," Andrew said, walking down the aisle to meet her.

"I think I would like that," she smiled.

Andrew led her to the front pew, where they sat and bowed their heads. After a prayer, Angie looked at Andrew.

"I still don't know if I believe," she said.

"The main thing is, does it help?" Andrew said, as he caught hold of her hand and helped her up.

"Oh, it helps a lot," she replied, smiling at him.

Julie was on her way back to the lodge when a car passed her so quickly that she had to jump into the hedge to avoid it. Julie thought she would call in and just make sure Sarah was all right, but when she got there, Sarah was not in, and there was no car there.

George and Jenny came down from the barn; they had been up playing with the tame owl. John and Sarah had gone to see some pigs, according to George. "Two men been," Jenny said. "Two nice men - we showed them owl, and told them about robin."

"Who were these men?" Julie asked.

"I don't know; nice men gave me this." Jenny held up a five-pound note.

"I don't expect any harm was done, but you shouldn't talk to strange men, especially if they give you things," Julie said firmly.

"Julie cross," Jenny said with a sad face.

"No, Julie not cross," she replied, as she put her arm around her and smiled.

Chapter Five

The following day Julie went up to see Angie and asked if she wanted to go for a walk.

"I can't," Angie replied. "I still don't want anyone to see me."

"Why, no one knows you here?" Julie said, trying to persuade her.

"In my game, you would be surprised who knows you," Angie replied with a smile.

Julie smiled back. "There is a place I would like you to see. Amy would like it, and we can go up across the fields - we won't see anyone."

"Okay then. If you are sure no one will see us, I'll come."

They left the cottage and made their way up to Julie's meadow. "It's not quite as good as it is when the flowers are out," Julie said, "but it is surely a magnificent place."

They made their way over to the pool with the stream running through it; Amy was running through the grass. There were three or four cows with their calves beside them; one was sucking from its mother. They got to the pool and sat down - the birds where singing.

"My, this is beautiful," Angie said, as she sat on the grass.

"This is where I spend a lot of my time; this is the place I fell in love, or where I knew it was love anyway."

"Do you believe in God?" Angie asked quietly.

"Yes, I believe. Do I believe in God in the way that Andrew preaches about him? That's a different story."

"How do you mean?" Angie said, looking puzzled.

"Well, some people pray when they go to bed, and some people pray before meals. I pray up here. I don't think God would have wanted people to spend money on building churches, although I'm glad they did; they are beautiful places, and so is this. But this didn't cost a penny; God made it for free. This is my church." Julie stretched out her arms.

"I quite like that," Angie replied. "Is there anything else you disagree on?"

"Only one thing - I believe that when we die, we return as something else. Hence all the birds around us - but I suppose that's not that different than Andrew. He believes that if we are good, we will all meet in heaven. Just look around you. Who's to say this is not heaven?" Julie said, as a little bird came right up to her as if to say, *you're right.*

"It sounds like you and Andrew don't get on?" Angie said.

"Far from it; I think he's a lovely man. I think of him as a great friend," Julie said with a smile.

"I think he's quite nice," Angie said, as she smiled back.

"Is that why you spend so much time there?" Julie asked, teasing her.

"No, it's just the church. It reminds me of my childhood and the good times in my life. Sometimes I just pray I could turn the clock back."

"That's something we can never do, but we can hope for a better future."

"I do hope so for Amy's sake, but I just fear he will find us."

"Who will find you?"

"The man I lived with - he might not worry too much about me, but he will miss the two thousand pounds I took with me."

Julie gulped. "Two thousand pounds?"

"Yes. It was me who earned it," she replied.

"I won't ask how," Julie said with a smile.

"Let's hope all that's behind me now," Angie replied.

"You said church reminded you of your childhood, so where did it all go wrong?"

"I never knew my mother. She died when I was a baby; my aunt brought me up until I was about ten, I think. She was wonderful to me. She never married, and it was just me and her."

"What happened then?" Julie asked, as she looked at the sadness in her eyes.

"My aunt died, and I went back to live with my father; he had never been to see me the entire time I lived with my aunt. I didn't know him," Angie sighed, tears starting run down her cheek.

Julie put her arm around her. "Don't upset yourself," she said.

"It's all right," Angie said, drying her eyes. "I don't know the last time I cried. I think I had forgotten how."

"Was your father bad to you? Is that where your troubles started?" Julie asked, thinking Angie might feel better if she got it out.

"Troubles - is that what you call it? The first couple of years were fine; he was out every night, and I was left home alone. I always heard him come home drunk, but I was in bed, so I never saw him. Then the night of my fourteenth birthday, I had had some school friends around. It was late when they left. I had spilt some Vimto down my top, so I took it off and washed it. My aunt always said that when I wasted something, I should wash it out right away."

Angie was getting hesitant with every word. Julie could see this as she asked, "Are you sure you want to go on with this?"

"I have never talked to anyone about it before. I think it might help if I get it all out; you might not want to be my friend afterwards, though."

"I don't think that whatever happened will make any difference to our friendship. That's one thing my parents taught me - never judge anyone."

Angie continued: "That night I washed my blouse out, put my nightie on and came and cleared up the room downstairs. My father came in drunk. He said I was a big girl now. He came over and put his hands over my hair. He said I should give him a birthday kiss; he was stinking of drink. I can smell it now. He fondled my breasts. I was quite endowed for my age. I kicked him hard on the shin and ran upstairs to my bed. I lay there thinking that was the end of it, when the door burst open, and he was there naked in the doorway. He came over and forced himself on me. This went on for about two years. Some nights he came home so drunk that he went right to bed. I prayed for those nights. He told me he was a war hero, and if I told anyone, they wouldn't believe me. Little did I know then that he never went to war - no, he was home shagging every woman on the street while their husbands were away fighting."

"How did you get away from him?" Julie asked. She passed her a hanky, as Angie's face was quite wet with tears.

"One day I just ran out of the house. I lived on the streets as a tramp for God knows how many years - going to the back of restaurants and eating food that had been thrown out. I slept anywhere I could, in old sheds or in the park - almost anywhere."

"That must have been awful," Julie said, as she put her arm around her.

"Things didn't get much better; one cold night I was hungry and freezing. I thought I was going to die, when this man approached me. He asked me if I wanted a bed for the night. I was so cold that it never entered my mind what I was letting myself into. He took me back to this big house. There were three other girls sitting on a large couch; they seemed friendly. The man suggested I have a bath. He gave me a robe to put on and said I should join them afterwards."

"It sounds like your knight in shining armour came along to your rescue," Julie said, still with her arm around her.

"That's what I had hoped, but I came down from my bath, and there were three men there, as well as the man who had brought me there. One of the men came over. 'She's new,' he said. 'How much for her?' The man who brought me there told him I was not ready yet, but he was taking bookings for me. Another man came over; he put what must have been twenty-five pounds on the table. 'I'll take her now,' he said, 'ready or not.' 'She might give you a bit of a fight,' said the man who brought me there. The man then took me to a room and raped me; it was a bit of a fight all right." Angie raised a small smile as she finished her story.

"How awful! What happened then? Did you go back on the streets to live?" Julie asked, as she threw a stone in the pond to keep Amy amused whilst Angie continued.

"I tried to get out of the house, but all the doors were locked; the windows had shutters that were all locked. I was a prisoner there. Every night men came around; if I didn't do what they wanted, I had a beating. I held out for about six months, but I got tired of the beatings. So I just gave in and became a professional prostitute - and hated every minute of it."

Amy came over, and Angie stood up, picked her up and swung her round and round.

"Where does she fit into the story?" Julie asked.

"Do I know who her father is? I haven't a clue - could be anyone from a lord to a shopkeeper," she said, as she put Amy down.

"Did you stay in the house and have her?" Julie was even more inquisitive.

"They couldn't let me out, as they knew I would spill the beans about what was going on. Besides, heavily pregnant women turn some men on."

"That makes me feel sick," Julie said angrily.

"Oh believe me, it made me feel sick. I must have been in that place over ten years - never went outside and hated every minute of it."

"How did you get out?" Julie asked, as they both started to walk a little farther across the field. Amy was chasing a little mouse that was running across the meadow.

"A man had come in off a foreign boat; he stank as if he were rotten. He was completely covered in scabs, and I refused to go with him. For refusing, I took one hell of a beating from the man we all had to call 'Boss'. He was the man who had brought me there. Anyway, there was a man who was with one of the other girls. He heard me screaming and came in my room. 'Don't beat her,' he said. 'I will pay you double if I can have her,' he said. Boss hit me again hard. 'You have her then,' he said and left the room. The man cleaned me up with his hanky. He asked me why I stayed there; I don't think he believed that I couldn't leave at first, but when he did believe me, he said he would help me.

"How did he do that?" Julie asked.

"He put himself in great danger," Angie continued. "He visited me a number of times, and then one night he said he had arranged a cottage for me and Amy. He said I had to be ready to leave at eleven thirty the next night. There would be a taxi on the corner to take me to the cottage. I asked him how he was going to do it. He said, 'Just trust me; you will know.' When he left, he said it would be the last time he would see me. The next night I went up to my room at about eleven fifteen, got Amy out of bed and packed her clothes. Then suddenly, there was one hell of a commotion. I looked downstairs, and the place was full of police. I took Amy and walked down the stairs. I walked right past the police, and no one challenged me. On the table by the door was a shoe box that Boss kept money in. I picked it up and walked out the door. There on the corner was a taxi, and I got in. He brought me here, and that's it, really."

"Who was that man?"

"I don't know - the only thing I can think of is that he was high up in the police. Why else would they let me pass?"

"What an awful life you have had! Well, I tell you what - we will make it a good life from now on."

"You're so kind," Angie replied.

"It must be awful doing it with just anybody; I can't bear to think of doing it with anybody other than my Fred. He makes me full of excitement, and my whole body tingles," Julie said, as they opened the gate.

"Nothing like that - no feelings - just a job you hate," Angie said, as they reached the farmyard.

"I hope one day you will be able to put all the bad memories behind you," Julie said.

Angie leaned forward and kissed her on the cheek. "Thank you," she said, as she left and made the short trip to the cottage.

Chapter Six

Julie had forgotten all about the men George and Jenny said they had seen. It was Sunday morning when Sarah phoned down to Julie at the lodge, asking if she had seen the Sunday paper.

"No," Julie replied.

"Well, I think you should get up here now and have a look."

Fred and Julie went straight up to the farm and went into the kitchen, where Sarah had the paper laid out on the table.

"You're in for a shock," she said before Fred and Julie got in the door.

Fred and Julie sat down at the table beside each other, and John and Sarah sat opposite. Julie could see the headline: WEST COUNTRY JUROR WAS VICTIM'S EX-LOVER.

"How can they say those things?" Julie asked, as she put her head in her hands.

"You'll want to read all of it," Sarah replied, as she got up from the table and put the kettle on.

Fred picked up the paper and started to read it.

After the headline, it continued:

A West Country juror knew the victims in a double murder case. He had a previous steamy relationship with one of the victim's daughters, alleges our informant, who is a well-respected local resident. Sarah Page, as she was then known, very often bunked off school to be with her lover Lenard James. Sarah is now married to John Brite at Tremarrow farm in a sleepy Devon village. We decided to go to Tremarrow farm after the informant told us that things aren't quite right there. He called it the funny farm - and after visiting the farm, who am I to argue?

I drove to the farm and was met by the owner, who we were led to believe was called John, but he introduced himself as George. He looked and talked like someone who lived in a turnip field. Then, a woman appeared, who I believe to be Sarah. She giggled at every question I asked and never once denied the fact that Lenard James was once her lover, so we have to assume it is true. I did feel a little sorry for them, as they should be in an asylum rather than a farm, especially when an owl flew on to George's shoulder and he introduced it as his mother. Then when a robin appeared, there was an argument between them, whether George was an uncle to it, or it was a sister to Sarah.

At this moment, I took my leave. I believe that we as a paper should fight for the freedom of Rupert Trelivan, and it is our duty to inform the local authorities regarding the two residences of Tremarrow farm, as I do not believe it safe to have people like this having sexual relations with anyone. We will be investigating whether any laws were broken when the girl - as she was then a simpleton - had a sexual relationship with Lenard James.

"Bloody hell!" Fred exclaimed, as he put the paper down.

"I don't know what to say, whether to laugh at it or get bloody mad," Julie said, picking up the cup of coffee Sarah had made.

There was a sudden shout from the door. It was Cart followed closely by Olive. "Have you seen this!" he shouted, as he entered the kitchen and banged the paper on the table.

"We certainly have," Sarah answered.

"How can they say these things? If I see the bugger, I'll rub his bloody nose in a turnip field."

"Oh, I forgot to say," Julie said with a smile, "George and Jenny said they had a visitor the other afternoon."

"Oh, the penny's dropped," Olive said, as she just realised it was George and Jenny they saw.

"I wonder who this informant is they talk about," Cart said, as he scratched his head.

"We know who the informant is. It's Brian Furze," John said, as he got up to put his empty cup in the sink.

"That bugger! We should go up to Princetown and ask him what his game is," Cart said angrily.

"We shouldn't do anything like that; we must leave it up to Mr Knight. I expect he will come up tomorrow," Sarah said, trying to calm the anger in the room.

"How will you feel facing people, dear?" Olive asked Sarah.

"That won't bother me; I know, and the people who matter to me, know that the things in the paper aren't true."

"Good for you," Julie replied. "Anyone who thinks differently will have me to answer to," Julie said with a smile.

Cart and Olive left, and the others stayed chatting for a while before Julie and Fred left to see to the visitors.

Over at the church, Angie was out early and was in the church saying a little prayer, as she now did most days. And most days, Andrew was there at the same time, not by coincidence. He liked seeing her. "How are you my dear?" he said, as he entered the church.

"I feel better than I have for years; I have found a good friend for a change," she replied.

"Oh, and who is that?" Andrew asked, hoping it was him.

"Julie, she seems a remarkable person," came the reply.

"She certainly is; I hold her as a very dear friend."

"She speaks very highly of you," Angie said.

"I'm glad. What about you? Do you regard me as a friend?" Andrew asked, in a way that brought a smile to her face.

"Oh yes, but you might not want me for a friend if you knew my former life."

"Oh, I think I would. If you want to get it off your chest, I'm here to listen you know," Andrew said, as he gently touched her hand.

"I told Julie my whole life story, and I think it helped."

"It usually does. Nothing is ever as bad as it seems," Andrew said, trying to reassure her.

"You know that I was a prostitute, don't you?"

Andrew went bright red. "I think I had worked that one out," he replied, "but I'm not here to judge."

"It was not by choice; it's quite complicated. There is one thing I would like to know - the man who helped me, did he get into trouble after the raid? He was obviously married. I also wonder - did the place get closed down?"

"I don't know, but I could ask a question or two if you like." Andrew so wanted to help her.

On Monday, Mr Knight came up and saw Sarah about what was in the paper. He suggested that she and John should meet the journalist and put out their side of the story. He said that if the reporter didn't turn up, he had a friend who was a journalist for a rival tabloid.

Sarah agreed, and Mr Knight made a couple of phone calls; a meeting was arranged for Wednesday.

Mr Knight had left when Julie came up to see Sarah. They both decided they would walk up to Julie's meadow; Julie suggested that they call on Angie, as she wanted Sarah to meet her and Amy. They walked up towards Angie's as she was just coming out of the church.

"I'd like you to meet my friend," Julie said, as they arrived at Angie's door together.

"Please to meet you," Angie replied. "I have heard all about you."

"That's more than I can say about you," Sarah replied with a smile.

"We are going up to the meadow for a walk and thought you and Amy might want to come."

"Love to," Angie replied. "I'll just put Amy's shoes on."

They made their way up to the meadow. Amy was

running around. Before they had come here to live, she had only been outdoors twice, and that was with one of the girls who could be trusted to go out.

They were all laughing and joking; it was as if Angie had known them for years. "Has Julie told you about my life?" she asked Sarah.

"Why would I? It's not for me to say; you might not have wanted her to know," Julie said before Sarah could answer.

Sarah and Angie sat down beside the pool. Julie went over to a biscuit tin she kept near the pool and took out three candles. She brought them over to where Angie was telling her life story to Sarah.

When she had finished, Julie gave them both a candle. "We will light one each to the future," she said cheerfully. She paused and said, "Oh, wait a minute; I better get another one for Amy." She went to the tin and got one more for the child.

"I'm so lucky," Angie said. "I could not have come to a better place - you two are wonderful, and Andrew the vicar, he is marvellous. I go to the church every morning to thank God for bringing me here. I'm never there long before he comes in. I think he only comes in to make sure I'm all right."

"Oh, I'm sure he has a soft spot for you," Julie said with a smile.

They all lit there candles and made their way back, and then Sarah asked them all in for some lunch.

After lunch, Angie and Amy made their way home. When they got to the cottage, they were met by Andrew. "Had a nice walk?" he asked, as they walked up the path towards him.

"Very good, thanks," Angie replied with a smile.

Amy asked, "Do you know we saw lots of birds and big cows?"

"Do you like the birds?" Andrew asked, as he crooked down beside her.

"Yes, but I like the cows best; they have babies. Do you know they drink milk from their mummies?" Amy asked, as she bent forward laughing.

"Do they?" Andrew replied. He was quite taken up with her.

"She had never seen an animal before we came here," Angie said, as she bent down, picked her up and cuddled her.

"I have come to give you a bit of news; they have not closed down the house that you were in. They found no evidence apparently, just a small amount of drugs in one bedroom."

"Some of the girls took drugs; they said that it helped them. In fact, some of the trusted girls said they enjoyed what they were doing, and the drugs enhanced their experience." Angie had tears in her eyes as she spoke.

Andrew put his arms around her and cuddled her into him. "Don't upset yourself," he said.

"Did you know that the entire time I was on the streets, I saw people steal from shops to get money for drugs as well as food - but for all that I have been through, I have never stolen anything or taken drugs," Angie said proudly.

"Someone somewhere must have taught you right from wrong," Andrew said, as he knelt down beside Amy. She had brought over a book with a picture of a cow to show him.

"I think it was my aunt; she was wonderful to me," Angie said. This brought another tear and another cuddle from Andrew.

Andrew left and went back to the vestry.

Chapter Seven

It was Wednesday morning, the day to meet the journalist. Sarah was feeling quite nervous. Julie was up quite early, and Mr Knight arrived not long after. He had a journalist with him from a rival newspaper. They sat down around the long kitchen table, with John and Sarah beside each other on one side of the table and Julie beside Sarah. Mr Knight sat on one end, and the reporter sat at the other.

They talked about what Fred had done down at the lodge, how John and Sarah had given the building, and how they had paid for all the building work.

"That's not all," Julie said. "Last Christmas they paid for all the food and all the residents stayed for free." She wanted to make sure the reporter knew how good John and Sarah were.

Then a car pulled into the yard. No one got out immediately - they waited until George and Jenny had come down from the barn to see the car, and sure enough it didn't take long before George was over by the car shaking the man's hand as he got out. Jenny was right behind him. George then led the man over to where the pigs were. "Is Mr Knight here?" the man asked, as George picked up one of the piglets and tried to hand it to him.

"My pig," George said quite excitedly. John had taken the piglet away from its mother, as she had fifteen piglets, and the other ones wouldn't let this one feed.

Julie then produced a baby bottle full of milk from her pocket. She took the piglet from George and started to feed it with the bottle. "George and Jenny's baby," she said.

The others were watching from the kitchen window and laughing at the expression on the man's face. "Someone better go and rescue him," Sarah said, as she laughed out loud.

"I'll go," Mr Knight said. "You all sit down; we might see a different expression on his face in a minute."

Mr Knight went out and led the journalist (who had written the scathing article) into the kitchen. When he got to the table, Mr Knight said, "You know Mr and Mrs Brite, I believe," he said, pointing to John and Sarah.

The journalist gulped. "You are Mr and Mrs Brite?" he said with some surprise.

"That's right. I'm the simpleton that shouldn't be having sexual relationships with my husband. And you are?" Sarah said angrily.

The journalist went bright red. "What can I say?" he replied in quite a light-hearted way.

"I should think you could start with sorry," Julie said angrily.

"Oh, I made a slight mistake, but it doesn't alter the fact that a man is in jail who shouldn't be," the journalist replied, showing little concern.

"If that's the way you think, then you better leave. You are just wasting our time," John said, as he got up and went to open the door.

"Now hang on," Mr Knight said. "I think there are a few things we need to get straight first."

John returned to the table and sat down. "Very well," he said.

Mr Knight continued. "Before we issue your paper with a writ, we will tell you the facts and give you the chance to write a withdrawal next Sunday."

"I doubt we will do that," the reporter replied.

"Just sit there and listen," Mr Knight shouted angrily. "We will start with Brian Furze. Did you know he has had more convictions for stealing and fraud than you have had hot dinners? The last time he went to jail, the judge told him it had become obvious that he was a compulsive liar."

"So how does that change things?" the journalist asked.

"How does that change things?" Julie said angrily. "I will tell you how it changes things - everything that man told you was a lie."

"So none of you knew Lenard James then - is that what I am supposed to believe?" the journalist asked in a sarcastic tone.

"No, that's not what you are expected to believe. No one has ever denied that, but Sarah has never had any relationship with Lenard James. That's one of the things that needs to be withdrawn," Mr Knight said firmly.

"I won't withdraw that, as I have only reported the facts as I have been told them by Mr Furze; they are not my words; they are his."

"That's it," John said. "Write what you bloody want to; now get up and get out of my house before I throw you out!"

This was the first time anyone had seen John lose his temper.

The journalist left. "What an awful man," Julie said, as he walked out the door.

"What happens now? Do you think we have made matters worse?" Sarah asked Mr Knight.

The journalist Mr Knight had brought said, "Don't worry; I will write a good story, and I will also expose his paper and him. I will even include this meeting. By the time I have finished, he will wish he had printed a retraction."

They all thanked the reporter and Mr Knight as they said their goodbyes.

After they had gone, Olive and Cart came over to see how they had got on.

"Good thing I didn't see him," Cart said, "or I would have broken the bugger's neck!"

"I think you probably would have," Julie said, as she started to laugh.

"By the way," Olive said, "how's the lady in church cottage settling in? I'd ask Andrew, but he doesn't say much about her."

"She's fine," Julie said. "I can't go into it, but she has had a terrible life; we should all work together to make her future something special."

"Well dear, you can count me in on that," Olive said, as Cart was leading her out the door. He wanted to get back and help Jan with a pig house they were building. Cart was as pleased as Jan that John had given over the ground for the traditional farm.

"I tell you what - see if she wants to go in to Tavistock on Friday. We could all go and make a day of it. I know Cart and Jan are going in. There are some sows for sale at the market that they want to buy."

"We haven't mentioned that to John yet," Cart said.

"Me and my mouth," Olive said with a laugh.

"You know, I will go along with what you want," John said. "Jan's the expert."

"I'll ask her, but I don't expect she will," Julie said as they left.

Julie said she also had to go. "Poor old Fred will think I have deserted him," she said as she kissed Sarah on the cheek.

Julie thought she would just nip over and mention Tavistock to Angie.

"I don't know; I would like to, but I'm not sure. Let me think about it; I will let you know tomorrow," Angie said with a smile.

"Oh, there is one other person coming. Olive, you will like her. She lives with Cart. She's a big friend of Andrew's," Julie said, as she went off down the path.

The next day Julie thought she better spend the day with Fred and the visitors. She thought Fred might think she was neglecting him. Although it wasn't visible, things had been a little strained between them since the miscarriage.

The whole day Julie never left Fred's side. They went out with the tractor train first, and then they sat outside the lodge with the visitors. George and Jenny kept bringing down animals to show them. Fred and Julie could not stop smiling at each other - things where returning back to normal between them, so much so that in the evening they went for a walk and ended up in the shed at the top of the field.

The following morning, Friday, Julie was at the farm ready for their day out in Tavistock.

"Hi," Sarah said, as Julie walked in the door. "You are positively glowing," she said with a smile.

"Am I? It must be the rush up the hill," Julie replied.

"Oh really, who you trying to kid?" Sarah smiled.

"You're a proper bugger. You know me too well." Julie, too, had a smile.

With that, John arrived. "What are you two looking so pleased about?" he asked.

"Oh nothing, it's just Sarah being her silly self," Julie said, turning bright red.

"I think it's more like Fred and Julie are back to normal; I have missed that glow on your face lately," Sarah said, as she watched John go out the door.

"I know; we have been so silly. I blamed myself for the miscarriage and kept it to myself, and Fred blamed himself and didn't know how to talk about it. So do you know what we did?"

"Do I want to know?" Sarah asked with a large grin.

"We went up to the old shed and talked about it," Julie said, as she picked up a cloth and wiped Sarah's dishes.

"My John blames himself for your miscarriage, but you aren't going to discuss it with him in the shed," Sarah replied, as she laughed out loud.

Suddenly, there was knock on the door. "Come in!" Sarah shouted.

Angie and Amy walked in. "I've decided that I would like to come if that's all right," Angie said.

"Of course it is; we can all ride in with John. I told Olive we would meet her up at the market," Julie said, as they all made their way towards the car.

When they got to the market, Olive was already there. Julie introduced Angie and Amy to Olive, and then they made their way down to the town. Julie and Angie held Amy's hands and kept swinging her back and forth, with Amy laughing her head off. When they got to the toy shop, Julie bought Amy a doll.

Things were going well. Angie had bought some clothes for Amy. "I would buy some for myself, but I love the ones you let me have. I love them to bits," she said to Julie.

"I'm glad of that," Julie said, giving a little wink to Sarah.

"I want to buy you all lunch," Olive said. She looked at Angie. "Do you know, these two girls spoil me to bits! They changed my life, especially this one." She put her arm around Julie.

"What nonsense," Julie replied.

"Oh, I can quite believe it; she has helped me more than she knows," Angie said with a large smile.

"Come on; let's go in here," Olive said as they got to a restaurant.

They sat down, with Angie looking rather confused. "You look troubled," Sarah said.

"This is the first time in my life I have ever been anywhere like this," Angie replied.

"Well, have a look at the menu, and choose something special," Olive said. "We will make it a celebration."

"I'll go along with that," Julie said, as she handed Angie the menu.

They ate there meal, and there was no doubt they were having fun. The bottle of wine had certainly given Julie the giggles. They started to walk back down the street towards the market, when suddenly they heard someone calling them.

"Oh look, it's Elsie, Andrew's sister," Olive said, with a bit of excitement in her voice.

They all stopped and started chatting. "They tell me someone has moved into church cottage," Elsie said.

No one answered, but then suddenly Angie said, "It's me - I have moved in."

"I'm very pleased to meet you my dear, and where do you come from? I don't think I have seen you around before."

Angie paused, not really knowing what to say, and then Julie quickly said she used to live in Plymouth. "She is an old friend of mine, and she belongs out here in the country."

"No wonder she got the cottage if you had something to do with it; Andrew always had a soft spot for you," Elsie said, with a tone of disapproval. With that, Elsie's husband appeared on the scene. "Oh, here's Arnold," she said, "I've been chatting too long."

"Hello girls," he said. Then suddenly he took a large gulp and started to splutter.

"Whatever is it dear? You look like you've seen a ghost," Elsie said.

"Just a bit of indigestion, dear," he said, as he turned his back on everyone and started to cough.

"We'd better be going," Elsie said. She said her goodbyes. "Remember me to Andrew." She turned and walked away with Arnold, who never turned to look back.

"Arnold was a bit funny, don't you think?" Sarah asked.

"Funny bugger; he is all right. We aren't good enough for him," Olive said with a smile.

"Why Olive, fancy you swearing; we don't hear that very often," Julie said with a smile.

"Well, he's enough to make you; I don't know why people vote for him - chairman of the town council, chairman of the district council, and a bloody magistrate - who the hell does he think he is?" Olive was really mad.

"Olive, I hope that's got it off your chest!" Turning to Angie, she said, "What do you think of our Olive, Angie?" She was surprised to see tears running down Angie's face. "What's the matter, Angie?"

"Oh, don't mind me," she replied. "I just want to get back now; it's been a long day."

They were soon at the market and met up with John, Jan and Cart, who persuaded them all to have a look at the two sows they had bought, which they did - pretending to do it with some enthusiasm.

They all made their way home. Amy was clutching her new doll. Angie didn't speak all the way home. The first thing she did when she got home was to go into the church to see Andrew. As usual, he was pleased to see her. She told him how she had met his sister.

"How is she? I don't see much of her since I fell out with that pompous husband of hers. I don't suppose you've met him?"

"Oh yes, I have," she replied.

They stopped and chatted for a while before Angie left to go into her cottage. Just before she went in the door, she could hear someone talking over the wall. She went and looked over, and there were Cart and Jan, sitting on a bale of straw admiring the two pigs they had bought.

"You pair want a cup of tea?" she asked.

"Proper job," was the reply.

Angie went in, made them tea and brought it out.

"You're going to fit in here proper," Cart said, raising his cup to her.

Angie smiled as she went back in. She thought Cart had a real friendly face for such a big man.

Chapter Eight

❧

Sunday soon came around, and John was out early to get the Sunday papers. Julie and Fred and Cart and Olive were at the farm when John returned. They were all on tenterhooks at what they were about to read.

John had purchased three copies of both papers. He handed out a copy at random to each of them. The paper that ran the story the week before had the headline:

FREE RUPERT TRELIVAN

Last week we ran a story about a man who had been jailed with the help of a corrupt juror. We also reported on the farm where one of the victim's daughters lives. I was invited to the farm by the family's solicitor. Although I made a mistake the week before - I had actually met Sarah Brite's brother and girlfriend and not Mr & Mrs Brite as stated - I have not changed my opinion. I was first greeted by the brother and girlfriend, who tried to hand me a pig; the girlfriend claimed it was her baby, as she produced a bottle and proceeded to feed it.

I was then asked into the kitchen where the Brites and

their solicitor tried to convince me that they were all normal and that Sarah had never had a sexual relationship with Lenard James, but nothing they said convinced me of this.

After I left the farm, I stopped in the village and spoke to some locals. The whole place made me think I was at the Mad Hatter's tea party. I was told about the lady who lived down at the lodge where the simpletons stay. Apparently this lady goes to a field that she calls a church; it was her that convinced people that all the animals were someone from another life. Oh, and the whole village saw an angel in a pond. I came away thinking that the entire the village should be locked up. I now know where the word *inbreeds* comes from.

The other paper had the headline:

THE KINDEST PEOPLE I HAVE EVER MET

After reading an article in a rival's paper last Sunday, I decided to investigate with an open mind. I first visited the farm, where I found some of the nicest people it has ever been my pleasure to meet. The whole place just seems to overflow with kindness. Sarah had an autistic brother, and she had looked after him since her mother died. Her friend Julie and Julie's husband Fred had taken in an autistic girl who had been living in a convent. Sarah's brother had never spoken until he met Fred, who spent hours teaching him. Sarah had inherited some money and some buildings. One of the large old mine buildings was turned into a holiday building for autistic people and their families, which is run by Fred. Not only did Sarah and her husband provide the building, Sarah paid for all the building work and equipment.

Sarah tried to play down what she had done and stressed that none of it would have been possible without Fred and Julie. She also stressed the help that the villagers had put in.

When I was in the farm kitchen, my rival reporter arrived, and I was there throughout his interview. It soon became clear that he did not want to address the fact that he had made an absolute blunder. All he wanted was a story. By story, I mean any story, even if it was fiction.

In his report the week before, he said Sarah had not attended school on some days to be with Lenard James, so I went and found her old headmaster, who turned out to be a meticulous person. Sarah had attended that school for four years, and he produced a register for each year, which showed one hundred per cent attendance. Sarah claimed that John had been her only boyfriend. I asked the headmaster if he had any views on that. He told me that it was pretty obvious how keen they were on one another at school.

This was something I also put to the local vicar, who had no doubt that there was only one man ever in Sarah's life.

I spoke to the family and local people at length, and I came away with three things on my mind. One, Rupert Trelivan is as guilty as hell. Secondly, the love and kindness at the farm and surrounding village is second to none. And thirdly, my competitor had stooped as low as any gutter press could possibly go.

Cart was the first to react after reading both articles. "I just don't know what to say. How can two people see it so differently? Surely, there is some law about printing lies. All of us who know you, we all know which story to believe. But what about other people?"

Sarah picked all the papers up. "I don't care what others think; the only people that matter know the truth, and that's all that matters to me," she said, as she put the papers in the bin.

"That's right dear; that's the best way to look at it," Olive said with a smile.

Julie put her arm around Sarah, who put an arm around her. "You make me so proud to have you as a friend; that little bulge is thinking, 'Look at my mum'," she said, as she rubbed her tummy with her other hand.

Everyone had a laugh at that. "Do you need to go down and get the visitors breakfast?" Olive asked Julie.

"I sure do," she replied.

"I will come down and give you a hand," Olive said, as she got up from the chair.

"Tell you what - why don't you all come down for breakfast?" Julie said. "We only have ten guests, so there is plenty of room."

"I'll go along with that," John replied.

"Me too," echoed Cart.

They were all eating their breakfast when suddenly the door opened, and there in the doorway was Amy. She ran over to Julie. "I was looking for you," she said. She was clutching the doll Julie had bought her.

"Have you? What did you want me for?" Julie asked, as she picked Amy up.

"Baby dirty," she said, as she showed Julie her doll. She had put it down in a puddle.

"Never mind; we can sort that out. Now does mummy know where you are?"

"I don't know," was the reply.

No one had noticed that Jenny had gone until she came back with one of her dolls and three or four doll dresses. She gave Amy the dresses without saying a word; she just smiled.

"She has as big a heart as you," Olive said to Julie, as she helped take the dirty dress off the doll and put on one of Jenny's.

"Shall I take you home now?" Sarah asked Amy.

"Oh, can't I stay a bit longer? I will be good."

"You're always good," Julie said, as she bounced her on her knee.

"I'll run up and tell Angie were she is," Fred said, making his way to the door.

Fred was only halfway up the drive when he was met by Angie. "Have you seen Amy?" she asked, all flustered.

"Don't panic; she's down here. I was just coming up to tell you - come on down and have a coffee or something."

As they entered the lodge, Amy saw her coming. She picked up her dolly and hid it behind her back.

Angie came right over to Amy. "You mustn't go off like that; you must always see mummy first," she said quite angrily.

"It was my baby who wanted to come," she said. "She got

dirty and wanted to see Julie; it wasn't my fault. It was baby's fault," Amy said.

Angie picked up the doll and pretended to talk to her: "You are very naughty," she said. "You mustn't go off without telling me."

"She won't do it again Mummy," Amy said.

Angie bent down and gave her a kiss. "I know she won't," she said with a large smile.

"Are you going to stay and have some breakfast?" Sarah asked.

"I would love to, but I promised Andrew I would go to church this morning. So I better get up; I would like to go for a walk later if anyone's up for it."

"You can count me in," Julie said. "I will come up and call after lunch."

"Me too!" Sarah shouted.

"And I will see you in church in a minute," Olive said, as Angie and Amy left.

Angie and Amy went home to get ready and went to church. As they walked in the door, the congregation went quiet; they all turned around and looked at Angie. Then there was just a lot of twiddle-twaddle going around the church.

Andrew walked down the aisle to meet her. "Come up and sit here," he said, leading her and Amy to the front pews.

It was obvious from the way the congregation had reacted that they had found out what she used to do.

After the service, Angie waited for Andrew to see the congregation off. "How are you?" Andrew asked, as he walked back into the church.

"Very embarrassed after that reception," Angie replied.

"Don't let that worry you; people soon forget, but what do they know? What you did seems to have spread through the village like wildfire."

"Oh, I know how they know; it doesn't worry me what people say, but it does worry me that a certain person knows where to find me. I will have to move."

"I shouldn't let him worry you; there are plenty of people here who will look after you. I don't know why you don't go to the police," Andrew said, as he put his arm around her.

"You are such a sweetie, but you don't understand that there is more than one man involved; it's an underworld organisation involving drugs as well as everything else."

"I don't understand how people got to know. I'm sure that the friends you have made here wouldn't say anything."

"Trust me. I know no one here said anything. That's why I will have to move."

"Please don't. We can look after you. I know we can." Andrew cuddled her in close and kissed her forehead.

Amy was getting anxious. "Can we go now Mummy?" she asked, tugging Angie's arm.

"Yes dear, we will go and have some lunch. What about you Andrew - would you like to join us?" Angie asked.

"You know, I would love to," he smiled. "Just give me a few minutes to get out of my work clothes."

Angie went in and made lunch. It wasn't long before Andrew appeared in a tee shirt and jeans. "Is that really you?" Angie asked with a smile as she put the plates on the table.

"This is good of you," Andrew said. "I had a bit of stale cheese in mind for my lunch."

"I think we can do a little better than that," Angie replied. "I'm going for a walk with Julie and Sarah this afternoon."

Andrew didn't answer, but he hoped they could persuade her to stay.

When Julie and Sarah called for Angie, she and Andrew where sitting outside the cottage drinking a cup of tea.

"This is cosy," Julie said in a teasing way.

Amy had taken a chair over by the garden wall, and she was looking over the wall. "Come here," she shouted to Julie, as soon as she saw her.

Julie went over. "What is it?" she asked.

Jan was sitting down on the other side of the wall. He had some corn in a bucket. He kept putting some in his hand, and a brown chicken kept coming up and eating out of his hand. Every time the chicken pecked at the corn, Amy would laugh. "Julie," she said, pointing down to Jan. "Is that old McDonald?"

Julie laughed. "It might be," she replied.

Andrew left and they all set out on their walk. "Where we going?" Angie asked.

"You ought to know the answer to that by now," Sarah replied with a bit of a giggle.

"Let me guess - Julie's meadow," Angie replied.

"Got it in one," Julie replied, as she produced a handful of candles from her pocket.

"You must keep the ironmongers in business with all the candles you buy," Sarah said with a large smile.

The three of them and Amy walked up through the fields towards the meadow. "You are quite quiet today; is everything all right?" Julie asked Angie.

"Not really, things didn't go right at church today," she replied.

"What, you and Andrew have fallen out?" Sarah said, teasing her.

"No," Angie gave Sarah a friendly nudge. "Andrew's lovely. He is so easy to talk to and so understanding."

"I think I sense a bit of romance in the air," Julie joked.

"Don't be silly; I don't believe in romance. I think that's just another name for lust," Angie replied quite forcefully.

"Oh, I have to disagree there. I love my Fred, and I know he loves me - and what we do is love, not lust," Julie said with a large smile on her face.

"Yes, and you do a lot of it, don't you my dear?" Sarah said, as the three of them sat down beside the pool at the bottom of the meadow.

"That's for me to know," Julie replied, still with a large smile.

"Well, I never want a man to touch me in that way ever again. I just hate it," Angie said angrily.

Julie put her arm around Angie. "You poor thing; you feel that way because you have never found love. You never know - with a bit of luck, you might someday. I can never know what you have been through, or how you feel, but what I do know is making love to someone you love is the most wonderful thing in the world." Julie's eyes were glistening as she spoke.

"Anyhow, what was wrong at church today?" Sarah asked.

"It was obvious everyone knew what I was; the place was just full of innuendos and whispering. It made me feel embarrassed, but not only that - now they know where I am. They will come after me. I am going to have to move."

"Why, they can't make you go back. You are safe here with us."

"You don't know them. I took their money and they won't let that go. I don't care about myself, but they could do something to Amy."

"I don't know how people found out," Julie said with a big frown on her face.

"I know how they know all right," Angie said quite angrily.

"How then? I know it wouldn't have come from any of us," Sarah replied.

"I know that, but I would rather not say; it would be too embarrassing for someone."

"What, you mean someone we know knew you as a prostitute?"

"Let's just say he was an acquaintance," Angie said, as she took a candle from Julie and lit it.

"I don't know why you just don't go to the police and have it done with," Julie said.

"If only life was that easy - you don't know how deep it goes. They are gangsters. The man at the house, he wasn't the head man. He was afraid. It wasn't only prostitution they were into; it was drugs in a big way. I could probably point the finger at a lot of people."

"Gosh, it's like a different world to what we know," Sarah said, as a shiver went down her back.

"I don't want to move. I have made friends that I could never make anywhere else." Angie had tears in her eyes as she spoke.

"Why don't you come and stay with us?" Julie asked. "That would be a solution."

"No way am I going to put you in danger; it's my problem, not yours. But thanks anyway." Angie lit the candle she had taken from Julie.

"Well, I don't think you should do anything hasty; just think about it for a while, and just remember that we will help in any way we can."

"I know that whatever happens, I will never forget you all," Angie said, wiping her eyes.

Amy ran back across the meadow with a large bunch of flowers she had picked. She gave them to Julie. "Thank you," she said. "What have I done to deserve these?"

"You're Mummy's friend," Amy said, laughing. This brought a tear to all of them.

They lit all the candles. Julie looked at Angie and caught hold of her hand. "Now you must make a wish," she said.

"I know what to wish for," she replied with her eyes shut.

They left the meadow and slowly walked back to the farm. "Thanks for a wonderful afternoon," Angie said as they reached the point where they split up.

"Can I go and see old McDonald when we get home, Mummy?" Amy asked excitedly.

"Oh I expect so," Angie replied with a smile.

Sarah went home and got John, and they both went down to the lodge to see Julie and Fred. Sarah wanted to know if Julie had any ideas about who might have visited a prostitute.

Julie said she had no idea. Fred suggested they go out for a drink that night and just see who was a likely candidate; they all agreed.

That night after all the chores were done, the four of them went down to the pub. Cart and Olive were already there when they arrived. They ordered drinks and sat back in the corner. They were chatting away when Gilbert Lane shouted out to them.

"Y'er you know that maid up church cottage?" he said.

"Yes, what of it?" Cart replied.

"Well they tell me she's a prostitute. Do you know how much she charges? I wouldn't mind a few shillings worth me self!" Gilbert said. Then he turned and laughed.

There was the loud noise of a chair scraping across the floor as Cart got up. He went over and picked Gilbert up by the scruff of the neck. "How long have I known you?" he asked.

"Fifty odd years," Gilbert stuttered.

"Every one of those years I wanted to break your bloody neck for something, but I've resisted. But make no mistake; if I hear that you have slagged that lady off again, I will break your bloody neck."

"All right; keep your hair on," Gilbert replied. He was shaking like a leaf. He crept back into the corner and no one heard a sound from him for the rest of the evening.

The evening ended with them all going home, none the wiser as to who could have known Angie and let the secret out.

Chapter Nine

Over the next few days Julie, Sarah and Olive spent a lot of time with Angie and Amy. It was like they were afraid to let them out of their sight. Amy took a chair out of the cottage at every chance she could and took it over by the wall, so she could watch Jan and Cart with the animals. Julie, Angie and Olive were all sitting outside the cottage when a red hen flew up from where Jan and Cart were. Amy ran over and got a biscuit, and within a few moments, the red hen was eating the biscuit out of her hand.

Julie said she had to go to get the teas ready at the lodge. Olive said she would give her a hand.

"Can I come?" Amy asked, in a way that no one could have said no.

"Of course you can, if Mummy says it's all right," Julie said, as she held her hand out for Amy to catch hold of.

"I don't mind," Angie replied. "I want to go and have a chat with Andrew about my future."

Amy went down to the lodge with Julie and Olive. As soon as she saw George, she knew he would show her an animal or two. "George, George!" she shouted, letting go of Julie's hand and running towards him.

George's face lit up when he saw her, and it wasn't long before Jenny came on the scene. She too was full of excitement.

George opened the gate, and he and Jenny caught hold of Amy's hand and led her down to the sheep. Julie and Olive watched them all the way. "I hope they don't move away," Olive said sadly.

Up at the church, Angie had gone in to see Andrew. She wanted so much to stay, but feared for her and Amy's safety.

Andrew told her she should do what she thought best. He would help her to move if that's what she wanted, but he also stressed that she would be sadly missed.

As they both left the church, their eyes were drawn to a black Jaguar parked across the road. Andrew commented that it seemed a bit posh for around here.

Angie left and walked the few yards to her cottage. She had just unlocked the door when she was grabbed from behind. She screamed loudly.

Andrew heard the scream and came running over. The man grabbed Angie by the hair and hit her hard across the face.

"Where's my money bitch!" he was shouting.

"Leave her!" Andrew shouted as he entered the room.

The man pushed her to the ground hard. He turned and punched Andrew, who fell to the ground. The man started kicking and continued to kick him harder and harder, Angie crawled along the floor until she was beside Andrew.

"Stop it; stop it!" she pleaded.

"I'll stop when you give me my money!"

The force of the kicks was just evil.

"You can have your money, but please-please stop; you will kill him."

Cart and Jan were sitting over the wall just watching the pigs foraging around when they heard the commotion. Cart climbed up over the wall and burst into the kitchen. He grabbed the man by the shoulder. The man turned and punched Cart hard on the chin, but his hand bounced off as if it had hit an iron door.

Angie flopped down beside Andrew, who was lying motionless on the floor. Cart dragged the man outside and shouted to Jan: "Phone for an ambulance, and then the police!"

Jan's wife, who they all called "Mrs", came out. "Whatever is the matter?" she asked, as she saw Cart was holding the struggling man tightly.

"Can you go down and fetch Olive and Julie?" he asked. "But don't let Amy come up here."

"I'll look after her," Mrs replied as she sort of waddled down the road.

The man was struggling and struggling. "If you struggle much more you bugger, I'll give you something to struggle for," Cart said.

Angie came running out. "Where's the ambulance?" she shouted. She turned and ran back in beside Andrew.

As Julie and Olive came running up, they came across PC Roberts. "You better come with us," Olive said. She was panting so fast, she could hardly get the words out.

They all hurried up to the cottage. Julie and Olive ran inside. "Help him; help him!" Angie shouted. "He's not moving."

PC Roberts went over to Cart. "What's the fuss about?" he asked in an authoritative manner.

"Bloody assault, that's what!" Cart said. "Bloody assault."

"Right; then put the man down Cart. If you apologise to this man, we will probably say no more about it."

"Not me you silly bugger; this man has assaulted the vicar, and for all I know he might be dead."

"You hang on to him. I'll go for reinforcements," the PC said, as he turned and started to walk away.

"Come back here you bloody fool!" Cart shouted. "Let's have your handcuffs."

"Oh, you can't have them; they're police property," PC Roberts replied. "I can't possibly let you have them."

"I will be bloody assaulting you if you don't get over here and put those cuffs on him!" Cart shouted angrily.

PC Roberts walked over beside them very gingerly with his handcuffs in his hand. "I've never used these before," he said, as Cart held out one of the man's arms for him to put the cuff on.

"Now put the other one around the railings," Cart said, as he dragged the man over towards the church.

"We got him," PC Roberts said, as he fastened the cuff around the railings.

"Now go and get Sergeant Gibbs; tell him what's happened." Cart was talking to PC Roberts as if he were talking to a child.

Cart went into the cottage. Andrew was still lying on the floor, not moving. Cart lifted his head. "Pass me that cushion," he said to Olive, which she did. He placed it gently under the vicar's head.

It seemed like ages before the ambulance arrived, but when it did come, it wasn't long before they had Andrew on a stretcher and in the back.

"Can Angie and I come?" Julie asked.

"Of course," the driver replied.

"What about Amy?" Angie asked anxiously.

"Don't worry about Amy. I'll look after her," Olive said. "Don't you worry."

The ambulance sped off with its bell ringing. Due to the severity of the vicar's injury, the ambulance went straight to Freedom Fields Hospital in Plymouth.

Cart stayed at the cottage until Sergeant Gibbs arrived with the police van to take the man away.

"Do you know his name?" the Sergeant asked Cart.

"Afraid not," he replied. "But he's a nasty bit of work; I think it's touch and go if the vicar will live."

"Bloody hell, that's bad," the Sergeant replied.

Back at the hospital, Julie and Angie were told to wait in the waiting room. They waited for what seemed like hours. Angie was blaming herself.

"If I had never come here, this would never have happened," she said, sobbing.

"It's not you coming that caused it," Julie said. "It's the fact that you didn't go to the police, when everyone knew about you."

"I couldn't. I wish I could have, but trust me, I did think it for the best." Angie was still sobbing.

"Don't worry," Julie said, as she put her arm around her. "What's done is done; we can't turn the clock back. All we can do is pray for Andrew."

"I just don't know what I will do if anything happens to him," Angie said, as she started to dry her eyes.

The doctor entered the waiting room. "How is he?" Angie asked, as she jumped right up in front of the doctor.

"It's difficult to say; he is in a coma. There seems to be no unusual swelling around the head, although there is a massive amount of bruising."

"Can we see him?" Julie asked.

"Yes, but only for a minute. The best thing for him is rest. Even though he is in a coma, it would probably be better if he slowly came around, as that will mean less pressure on his brain."

The two of them gently opened the door of the ward. Andrew looked so peaceful. They slowly walked over and gave him a gentle kiss. The doctor was right behind them. "That's enough now," he said quietly.

The two of them left, and when they got to the waiting room, Fred was there waiting for them. They solemnly went out to the car. "Is Amy all right?" Angie asked.

"Full of excitement on Cart's shoulders, eating an ice cream last I saw," Fred replied.

When they got back, Julie and Angie went in to Cart's and Olive's place. Amy was fast asleep in the spare bed. "She can stay tonight if you like," Olive said.

"Are you sure? It seems a pity to wake her." Amy was oblivious to what was going on.

"You can stay down with us tonight," Julie said to Angie. "It might be better than going back to the cottage right now."

"I don't deserve friends like you," Angie said. She started to cry.

"Come now," Cart said. "We don't want waterworks; with what you've been through, you deserve good friends."

"You know, before I came here, I couldn't cry; now I seem to cry every day. Have I brought you all a lot of sorrow?"

"For goodness sake, you have not brought any sorrow; see the love you have brought. Amy has taken years off Olive."

"Charming. How many years is that then?" Olive asked, laughing.

"Oh, you know what I mean," Julie smiled. She turned to Angie. "What life did Amy have, or would she have had - how long before she would have been sexually abused if you had stayed there?"

"I know, but what about Andrew? He still might die, and it's my entire fault."

"Andrew is strong willed, and I'm sure he will pull through. But even if he doesn't, I know he would lay no blame on you whatsoever," Olive said, trying to reassure her.

"You are all so kind. I have made my mind up to one thing. Whatever happens, I am not moving, I'm here to stay," Angie said firmly.

"I'm glad to hear it," Julie said. "Now come on, let's go down and get some supper."

They left Cart and Olive and went down to Julie's place, where Angie spent the night.

They all went to the hospital each day to visit Andrew; there was no change in his condition. On the Friday of the first week, the doctor came to tell them that they were going to move Andrew back to Tavistock, as there was no more they could do.

"Will he get better?" Julie asked.

"I honestly don't know; it has been shown in the past that if you keep talking to someone in a coma, they do come out of it. That's another reason to move him to Tavistock. They have longer visiting hours and more visitors at a time, which might help."

Chapter Ten

Andrew was moved back to Tavistock on Saturday. The time it took to organise the move didn't leave much time for visiting, but they all agreed with Matron that they could all come in force on Sunday afternoon and spend the afternoon there.

On Sunday morning, they were all up early doing the daily chores, when Cart arrived at Tremarrow farm, waving the paper. "I thought we all agreed we wouldn't buy any more Sunday papers," Sarah said, as Cart entered the kitchen.

"I know, but I read the headline and couldn't resist it!" Cart said all excited.

Sarah took the paper from him and started to read it. The headline said:

OUR PAPER OWES AN APOLOGY TO THE BRITE'S AT TREMARROW FARM

It continued:

The other week we ran a story about a family and its village friends. The story was totally unjust, and we offer our unconditional apology. The story was produced by one of our journalists, and the views were his and his alone. Needless to say, he is no longer with our paper. Some of the language and wording used was totally unacceptable. Over the next couple of weeks, we will be contacting the couple to see how we can help them with the project they and their close friends Fred and Julie are involved in, helping people with autism.

"Gosh," Sarah said. "I wonder what that's all about. Do you think they really have sacked the journalist?"

"Well, I don't think they would say so if they hadn't," Cart said, as he put his arm around her.

"I must go down and show Julie," Sarah said. She was really excited. "Oh, do you mind if I keep it?" she asked Cart, realising she had taken his paper.

"No, that's fine love. I must get on. I've got a bit to do with old Jan, and then early lunch, as we have all got to go and see the vicar this afternoon."

"There seems to be a lot of old chatter going on at that little farm, with you and Jan," Sarah said as she gave him a big smile.

"Got to discuss things - us old folk spend a lot of time planning. Old Jan's got a lot of stories to tell. It's a job to stay away from him for a day." Cart had a big laugh as he spoke.

Sarah had taken the paper down to show Julie. Then she came back and got the lunch.

It was about one thirty when they all left to go to the hospital; they were all in the ward, including John, Sarah,

Fred, Julie, Cart, Olive, Angie and Amy. They all had chairs around the bed. Angie sat near Andrew's head. They were all chatting away, and Amy was sitting on Olive's lap.

They had been there about an hour talking to Andrew, going over everything that had happened in the past. They just hoped for a sign that he could hear them, but to no avail. He just lay there motionless.

The ward door suddenly opened, and there in the doorway was Elsie, Andrew's sister. "What's that whore doing here?" she screamed as she looked at Angie.

"Come Elsie, there is no need to get like that. Angie has as much right to be here as any of us," Olive said angrily.

"Really, you think so do you? None of this would have ever happened if it wasn't for that bitch," Elsie replied.

Angie turned towards her. "Whore am I, bitch am I? I've had enough!" she screamed. "It's time for some truths. You know whose fault it is that Andrew is in here - your bloody husband's, that's who!"

"Don't talk such nonsense! What can my Arnold have to do with it?" Elsie asked.

"What business is it that your husband's in? Do you really know? I bet you don't - try prostitution and drug dealing for a start!" Angie was really fuming.

"I have never heard such Tommy rot in all my life. My Arnold is the pillar of the community." Elsie was visually shaking.

"Bloody hell - Angie, is this true?" Cart asked, as he looked a bit bewildered.

"That day when we saw him in Tavistock - that's why he

turned away; he hoped I hadn't seen him. That's why when it got out, I knew where it had come from. But I didn't want to say because I thought it would embarrass Andrew." Angie started to cry as she spoke.

"What you mean? He used to have sex with you?" Julie asked, as she turned up her nose.

"What I mean is - he was the boss! He owned the place. He never had sex with me, but he did with some of the girls."

Angie had now calmed down.

"I think you should tell the police all this," Olive said, "for the sake of the other girls."

"I will; I feel so much better now that I have been able to say this, but none of this will help Andrew." As she was talking, Angie reached in the bed and caught hold of Andrew's hand.

"You're a liar as well as a whore!" Elsie shouted. "Now leave my brother alone and get out!"

"I'm going nowhere!" Angie shouted back. Then in a soft voice she said, "I'm staying here with the man I love."

Suddenly there was a slight stir in the bed and a very quiet voice said, "Say that again."

It was Andrew. He gently squeezed her hand. "Say what again?" she said softly.

"That you love me," he whispered.

Angie leaned in over the bed and kissed him on the forehead. "I love you, I love you, I love you," she said in a very soft voice.

No one had noticed that Cart had gone missing. Julie had gone for the nurse, and Olive had caught hold of Elsie's arm and had led her out to the waiting room, leaving just Sarah, Amy and Angie in the ward. "That was a bit of a surprise," Sarah said, as she came up beside the bed.

"I know. I am so sorry I couldn't tell you about Elsie's husband," Angie said. "I was afraid it would make it bad for Andrew."

"That's not the biggest surprise. I never trusted that slimy bugger; nothing would have surprised me about him - I mean you and Andrew." Sarah smiled at them as she spoke.

"I don't know that Andrew feels the same," Angie replied.

"Oh yes I do," came a quiet voice from the bed.

With that, the nurse entered the ward. "Things are looking good, I hear," she said, as she went over to the bed were Andrew was lying.

"Oh yes," Angie replied. Her face was just full of joy.

It wasn't long before the doctor arrived. "I will have to ask you to leave now," he said. "I expect you are all a lot happier now than when you came in."

"Can we come back later?" Angie asked.

"I would rather you didn't just at the moment. I know it's good to have him back with us, but I feel that too much excitement might not be good for the patient. We don't want that now, do we?" the doctor said.

"Can I just come back and say goodbye when you have done your examination?" Angie asked.

"If you wait in the waiting room, I will come and fetch you. It will be just goodbye mind." The doctor said giving her a little smile.

"Thank you," Angie replied as she smiled back.

Out in the waiting room, Olive was sitting down with Elsie, who was quite distraught. "I have been married for thirty years, and I don't know what business my husband is in. Just tell me Olive, it can't be true, can it? Tell me it's not true what she was saying in there."

"I'm afraid I can't tell you that, as I don't know, but she has not given me any reason to disbelieve her. Besides, don't you think it strange that you don't know what business he is in?" Olive asked as she held Elsie's hand.

"I can't get it out of my mind. I don't know what to do if it's true; it will ruin us." Elsie started to cry.

"Surely you would know if he had been with other women," Olive said, trying to comfort her.

"I wouldn't know. We might have been married for thirty years, but since he came back from the war - what, nearly twenty years ago now? - we haven't slept in the same room. The war changed him; our marriage has just been for show," Elsie explained. She looked at Olive. "Don't look like that," she said. "It suited me; I have never gone without."

"No - except for the very thing that mattered," Olive said.

"What's that?" Elise replied, looking surprised.

Olive looked deep into Elise's sad face. "Love, that's what," she said.

Angie and the others came into the waiting room. Elsie went right up to Angie. "Tell me, is it really true?"

"I'm afraid so," she replied. "God, I wish it wasn't, for Andrew's sake, but I'm afraid your husband is the main man behind everything that goes on. He and the others have ruined my life." Angie sat down beside Julie.

"I'm so sorry," Elsie said. "I'm such a fool. How could I have not known all these years?"

Julie put her hand out and caught hold of Angie's. "Your life is not ruined; it's just starting," she said, as she gently squeezed her hand.

It wasn't long before Cart came back in the room. No one had missed him.

"What do I say when I go home? Will you come with me Olive?" Elsie asked.

"No need to say anything," Cart said. "Arnold won't be there."

"Why? Where is he?" Elsie asked with some concern.

"When I left, he was trying to explain to Sergeant Gibbs why there was about a thousand pounds worth of drugs in the boot of his car," Cart said, looking pleased with himself.

"How does the Sergeant know?" Sarah asked.

"Because I went and got him," Cart said. "Didn't want the bugger running away."

"You can't really blame Arnold; it is all down to the war," Elsie said, trying to justify what he had done.

"The war! What the hell has that got to do with it? That was twenty years ago, and besides, Arnold never left these shores," Cart replied angrily.

"Oh yes he did. He was in intelligence. It was top secret what he did," Elsie said firmly.

"Top secret? If I remember rightly, he never left Plaster Down camp. You never believed then that he was selling stuff on the black market; he was robbing the yanks blind," Cart said. "I'm sorry Els, but I hope he gets everything that's coming to him."

It was then that the doctor came in to tell Angie she could go in and say goodnight.

"Can I come Mummy?" Amy asked.

Angie looked at the doctor, who gave a little nod.

After Angie had said goodnight, they all made their way home. Julie asked Angie if she and Amy wanted to come down and stay with them.

"Can I stay with Olive?" Amy asked.

"No darling - Olive doesn't want to be bothered with looking after you."

"Who says she doesn't?" Olive replied. "She is welcome to stay any time; it's a pleasure to have her."

"Well, if you are sure, it would help. I have a lot to get my head around," Angie said as she got in the back of Fred's car.

"We've got a lot to talk about," Julie said, as she got in the front.

Later that night after Fred had gone on to bed, Julie and Angie sat down with a cup of cocoa. "Now tell me all about this romance; I had no idea you and Andrew were a couple."

"Oh, I don't know what to say; it just came out. I do think I love him, but I don't know in what way. Does that make sense?" Angie took a sip of her cocoa.

"No not really; but carry on," Julie said, as she brought her legs up onto the settee.

"Well, he's kind; I know he cares for me. I know I get excited every day when I go and see him, and I know he is just as pleased to see me. But here's the problem - you know you told me how you feel when you make love? Well, I don't think I could make love with Andrew, or anybody, come to think of it. So does that mean I don't love him?"

"No, I would say it means your body has been abused; whether that will ever change, I don't know, but I hope for your sake it does. You deserve some real love."

"You don't think I have led Andrew on? Perhaps if he tries something, I should just lie there and let him do it."

"You should do no such thing. When he comes home, you should tell him how you feel, and tell him everything. If you want to be with him, you mustn't start off with a lie." Julie put her empty mug on the floor.

"I am so lucky to be here," Angie said. "I just hope this will be an end to my past. I don't know what to do with the money I took; I feel I should get rid of it. It's not really mine."

"Keep it; you bloody earned it, and besides, you and Amy have to live."

"I know, but I'm just afraid it will bring me bad luck," Angie said as she gave a big yawn.

"Come on," Julie said, "I think it's time for bed."

Chapter Eleven

It was another week before Andrew was allowed home. Angie had arranged a welcome home party with Julie's help. She had even gone and asked Elsie to come. It was a good sunny day; Fred had gone and picked him up.

Everyone sat out in Angie's garden, which joined the church. There was a large welcome home banner stretched between the church and cottage.

Sarah was on the other side in the cemetery, talking to her baby who had died, when Amy came over. "Who are you talking to?" she asked, as the only thing she could see was a robin on the gravestone.

"Oh, I'm just saying a few words to my baby," Sarah replied.

Amy looked behind the gravestone. "Where is he?" she asked. She sat down where Sarah was kneeling.

"She died," Sarah said, "but I feel she is here with us."

"Mummy used to say she wished she was dead; I don't want her to be dead," Amy said, as she screwed her face up.

"Don't worry, that won't happen. Mummy is happy now; she has had some very sad times," Sarah said. She sat down on the grass beside her and gave her a little cuddle.

"I've had some sad times," Amy said. "I lost my front tooth - look."

"That was very sad," Sarah said with a little smile.

"Sarah, if your baby is in the ground here, then Jenny told me a lie." Amy was looking really confused.

"How's that dear?"

"Well, you see that bird there? Jenny said that was your baby." Amy was pointing to the robin perched on the gravestone.

"Well, I think she might be right; he seems to follow me around," Sarah said. She stood up and caught hold of Amy's hands and pulled her up.

"I like that bird; he's very friendly," Amy said, as she got to her feet.

"Come on; we must go over with the others. Look, I think Andrew has arrived home." Sarah had hold of Amy's hand as they quickly went over to Angie's.

They got there just as Fred arrived with Andrew. There was a large cheer when he got out of the car; nearly all the village had come over to greet him, and much to everyone's surprise, Elsie got out of the car. She looked quite embarrassed when she saw all the people there.

Realising how awkward Elsie must be felling, Julie went right over and took her by the arm. "Come over and have a drink," she said, leading her to a table all laid out with drinks.

"I shouldn't have come, should I?" Elsie asked, as she picked up a drink off the table.

"Of course you should. I know it's awkward, and people will talk for a while, but that won't last long. After all, you can't shut yourself away." Julie put her arm around her shoulder as she spoke.

"I think I should - I haven't been to town yet; I just can't face people down there."

"The sooner you go out and meet them, the sooner they'll forget," Julie said, trying to reassure her.

"I know what you say is right, but it will be on people's minds until Arnold's case comes up."

"Do you know when that is?"

"No. I spoke to his solicitor yesterday. He thinks it could take months."

"Does he think he will go to jail?"

"That's definite; he thinks he will get ten to fifteen years if he is found guilty on all the charges they have now, but they are still looking into other things."

"Will he plead guilty?" Julie asked.

"That's the only way I will stand by him; I know what he has done is despicable, and I know our marriage has been a bit of a sham, but he has looked after me, and I can't forget that," Elsie said, trying to justify her decision to stand by Arnold.

"I just hope you get through it all right," Julie said. Elsie could see that she meant it.

"You know, Cart always said I had my nose so far up in the air that one day a seagull would shit on it, and that would bring me back down to earth. Well, it's certainly done that all right," Elsie said, looking sad.

The afternoon went well, with every one wishing Andrew a speedy recovery. But it soon became clear that

Andrew was getting tired, and it wasn't long before everyone had gone home, except Julie, Sarah and Elsie, who had gone into Angie's cottage to sit with Andrew while the rest of them cleared out. Amy had gone off with Olive again; she had really taken to her and Cart.

When the crowd had thinned out, Fred came up to take Elsie home. Julie and Sarah left, leaving Angie and Andrew in Angie's cottage.

"I think you should lie down," Angie said. She thought Andrew was looking very tired.

"No, I want to go for a walk," he replied. "I want to go up to Julie's meadow," he added softly.

Angie got her coat and the pair of them slowly walked up across the fields towards Julie's meadow. They hardly spoke, but as they got near the meadow, Andrew slowly slipped his hand into Angie's. They just looked at each other and smiled.

They walked over to the large pond. "Let's sit here a while," Andrew said, as he took off his coat and put it on the ground for them to sit on.

"It's beautiful here," Angie said, as she sat down beside him.

"I love it here. What is strange is that none of us found this place until Julie came here to live - what we had missed in all those years." Andrew caught hold of her hand again.

"She is someone special to you all, isn't she?" Angie replied.

"She certainly is, but the point I am trying to make is that you must think of yourself like this meadow - lost for years - but when you have been found, you just bloom."

"That's such a lovely thought," Angie said. She reached up and gave Andrew a kiss on the cheek.

"We have to talk about your future," Andrew said, looking rather stern.

"I want to spend it with you," Angie said. "I thought you wanted the same."

"Oh I do, but it's not about me. It's what's best for you; you have had a traumatic time, and your life is just beginning. You have to be sure you want to spend it with someone old enough to be your father."

"Hey, you aren't that old, and beside's I love you. I don't care how old you are."

"You can share your life with me either way, but are you sure you don't just look on me as a father you wish you had?"

"I don't know what I would have done if you had died. I feared that for the first time I had found love and it was going to be taken away from me. And it was all my fault."

"It's not your fault. When I think back, it's all of us around here that are to blame. During the war, we all knew what he was selling; he was stealing from the Americans, and we should have done something about it. Then, perhaps, your life would have been so much different."

"I feel sorry for your sister. Her life has been turned upside down. How will she cope?"

"Probably done her some good. When it all calms down, it'll bring her down to earth where she belongs. I would have thought you would be angry with her."

"That's what I don't understand. I can't get angry. Any anger I had has been drained out of me over the years." Angie had a little cry as she started to remember her past.

"I feel quite tired now. I think we should start to make our way back," Andrew said as he stood up.

"Wait. Before we go, I need to say something," Angie said, looking very serious.

"What is it?"

"You know I said I love you. Well - "

"What is it? Have you changed your mind?" Andrew had a note of nervousness in his voice.

"No, I would never do that. It's the physical side of the relationship - I don't know if I can do that." Angie turned her back on Andrew as she spoke.

Andrew had a little laugh. "Don't worry; we will still be good for each other with or without that."

"I sometimes think you aren't for real; it's no wonder I love you to bits. Now come on, let's get you back for a rest," Angie said as she helped Andrew put his coat on.

They soon made their way back home. Andrew went into the vicarage, and Angie strolled back to her cottage.

Chapter Twelve

A few weeks had passed. Angie and Andrew were getting ever closer, Sarah was getting quite big, and there was no more news of Rupert Trelivan's appeal. Amy had been going to the local school, and today was her fifth birthday, so a party had been arranged down at the lodge, which now doubled as Tremarrow Village Hall.

Lots of Angie's new school friends, their parents and even grandparents were invited. This was to be Amy's first ever party, and with the help of Julie and Olive, Angie wanted to make it a party to remember. The three of them went to Tavistock, where they went to Mr Creabers and bought all their cold meat and nibbles.

"No need to go anywhere else," Julie said. "We want the best, and this is the place to get it."

As they started to make their way back to Tremarrow, Angie suddenly said, "We have forgotten all about a cake."

"No we haven't; Sarah's making one. She's the best cook, so it was better left to her," Julie said with a large smile.

They were all soon at it, laying out the tables and blowing up balloons. The parcels were filled, ready for traditional games like pass the parcel. When everyone arrived, Cart took them all for a ride on the tractor train, and then it was back for a cold meat tea followed by jelly blancmange and then, of course, the cake. Now it was time for the games. Even the grandparents got involved; it really took them back to their childhood. It certainly was a party to remember; the look of excitement on Amy's face was a picture. That was until everyone was gone, and the clearing up was going on - Amy had sat up on a chair with her head in her hands.

"What's the matter?" Angie asked. "You look so sad."

Then Julie noticed how sad she was looking. "What is it dear? You have lots of nice presents, so why are you so sad?"

Amy started to cry. "Everyone has a Nan and Granddad except me," she said crossly.

"Never mind that; you've got Auntie Julie and Auntie Sarah, and then there's Olive and Cart and Andrew," Angie said. She picked her up and cuddled her.

Amy put on a little pleading smile when she looked at Olive. "Will you be my Nan?" she asked.

"I would like too," she replied. "And I know Cart would love to be a granddad."

"That's good then; this is the best party ever," Amy said, as her face lit up.

They all left and went home full of smiles. Angie put Amy to bed, as she was totally exhausted, and then Andrew came around to spend the evening with her. Andrew had been around for about half an hour when there was a knock on the door; Angie was in the kitchen making a cup of tea. "I'll go," Andrew shouted.

Andrew opened the door and was met by a man. "Could I speak to Angie please?" he said.

"Who shall I say you are?" Andrew asked.

"Oh, I'm sorry," the man said, as he opened his wallet. "Detective Sergeant Brian Steal," he replied.

"You better come in." Andrew showed the Sergeant into the front room.

"Who is it?" Angie shouted.

"The police," came the reply.

Angie quickly came into the room. "Oh, it's you," she said with a note of surprise.

"You know him?" Andrew asked, also with some surprise.

"Yes, this is the man that planned my escape, but I had no idea he was in the police force."

"I couldn't tell you; I didn't want to blow my cover. I do need to be perfectly honest with you; it was not a coincidence that you ended up here."

"What do you mean?"

"Well, we didn't know who was behind this, which can only be described as a massive empire of drugs and prostitution. I had found out from Lucy that the top man came from the Tavistock area."

Angie interrupted, "Lucy was one of the trusted girls; she could go out by day and do what she wanted. She seemed to enjoy the job."

"I don't know about that," the Sergeant continued. "We watched the house day and night, and we never saw him come or go."

"I don't know where the entrance was, but he never

came in the front door. He always came up from the cellar somehow," Angie told the policeman.

"Anyhow, when I saw how you were treated, I knew I had to do something to get you out of there, so I spoke to my friend the bishop because I knew they owned some property near Tavistock. And I thought if I could get you here, the chances are you would run across Mr Big and tell us who he is."

"I can't believe it! Do you know what danger you put us in? Do you know what happened to Andrew - how he was nearly killed?" Angie was fuming as she spoke.

"Hang on," the officer said. "I don't think that was anything to do with what we had done. It was more the fact that you took the money, and I don't think our Arnold knew anything about that."

"You're probably right. I shouldn't have done that," Angie said. She got the shoe box full of money and passed it to the officer.

"I don't want that," he replied quietly. "As far as we are concerned, that money never existed. Anyway, who's to say it's not yours?"

"If you don't want the money, what do you want?" Angie asked, as she moved the seats so that she was sitting beside Andrew.

"Well, our friend has admitted the drug dealing, but denies all the rest. I have two other girls that will give statements, and I hoped you would do the same."

"What do you think, Andrew?" Angie asked.

"It is entirely up to you, but if you want my opinion, I think you should. You know I'll support you either way."

"Yes, I'll do whatever it takes," Angie said. "By the way, did you know Arnold is Andrew's brother-in-law?"

"Yes, Sergeant Gibbs told me. Now do you want me to come out again and take the statement, or can you come in to the Tavistock police station?"

"I'll come in to the station if that's all right," Angie said. The policeman got up to leave.

After the policeman left, Angie finished making the cup of tea she had started. She and Andrew sat down beside each other on the settee.

"I'll be glad when this is all over, and I can put my past behind me," Angie said. She nestled in close to Andrew.

"You know I will always be here to help you," Andrew said, as he placed his arm around her.

"I do worry about what our future will be. Sometimes I think I'm in a dream, and I'm going to wake up and find myself back in that horrible house again."

"That's something that will never happen to you again. I will make sure of that."

"Do we have a future together? I can't imagine the bishop agreeing to you being with an ex-prostitute who is a single mother, and what would God think, let alone the parishioners?"

"Oh, you leave God to me; he'll be on our side. As for the bishop, I have already spoken to him, and he's fine. As for the parishioners, I think you would be surprised. I can't think of anyone who hasn't accepted you as one of us, as they say."

"You are so sweet Andrew. What did you say to the bishop? I wish I was there." Angie smiled.

"I told him all about you and your life. I also told him how I wanted to spend the rest of my life with you."

"What did he say?"

"He sort of frowned, then sighed, then said, 'I see.' Before he could say anything else, I offered my resignation."

"That's what I was afraid of; you can't do that for me," Angie said crossly.

"Whoa, whoa, hang on a minute. I didn't only do it for you – there are two people in this relationship, and I didn't care what would happen. The only thing I care about is being with you. Many years ago I was in love, but she didn't want me to go into the church. But I chose the church over her, so I think I have done my bit for God."

"What will you do? Where will you live?" Angie asked, looking at Andrew with concern.

"You should be asking, 'where are *we* going to live?', not asking where I am going to live." Andrew was smiling as he spoke.

"All right then, where are *we* going to live?"

"In the rectory if that's all right with you. The Bishop shook my hand and wished me all the best."

"You bugger," Angie said, "why didn't you tell me?"

"I was waiting for the right moment," he replied.

Angie turned towards Andrew and looked deep into his eyes. She could see so much love there. Their heads came closer and closer until they were locked in a long passionate kiss, which seemed to last and last.

When they broke away, Angie was physically shaking.

"Did God play a part in that?" she asked quietly.

"I don't know, but if he did, he certainly knows how to make a man happy," Andrew said with a beaming face.

"A girl too," Angie replied.

Andrew stayed a short while longer before going back to the vicarage.

The next morning Angie went over to the vicarage to see him while Amy ate her breakfast. She wasn't long before she was back to take Amy to school; then she went off down to the lodge to help Julie. This was her routine most mornings. She knew that as soon as Julie had finished the breakfasts and prepared the lunches, they could go for a walk, usually up to the meadow.

When Angie got there, Julie was at the sink doing dishes. She saw Angie come in; her face was absolutely glowing.

"Whatever are you looking so happy about?" Julie asked, as she plonked plate after plate on the draining board.

"How do you mean?" Angie replied, picking up a tea towel and starting to dry the plates.

"Well, you're looking like someone that just won the football pools."

"Better than that - last night I had the first kiss in my life that meant something. I never thought something so simple could have such an effect on me." Angie was just so excited.

"Our Andrew is a good kisser then, is he?" Julie asked, trying to tease her.

"Well, he is to me; he made my legs go to jelly. I just wish I could bring myself to let him have more," Angie said, as the smile left her face.

Chapter Thirteen

The dishes were done, and Angie and Julie were sitting outside of the lodge when Jenny came over to Julie. "Mummy," she said, "can I have another apple?"

"Of course you can dear, but that is the third one you have had this morning," Julie replied.

"I know. I wish I knew how many I had to eat," Jenny replied, looking rather puzzled.

"What do you mean?" Julie asked, looking rather confused.

"Well, how many apples do you have to eat to have a baby?"

Angie was just drinking her tea as Jenny said it. She burst into laughter and spat her tea across the yard.

"I don't think apples will make anyone have a baby," Julie said in a soft voice.

"Yes," she replied. "Cart told George."

"Told George what?" Julie asked, as she wiped an apple in her blouse and passed it to Jenny.

She took a big bite out of it, and then she said, "George asked Cart how babies got into tummies. He told George it was like apple trees; they grow from little seeds; when George asked him what a seed was, he cut an apple in half and took out these." She showed Angie and Julie the pips from her apple. "Cart said these were the seeds."

"That's right dear. These are apple seeds, and apple trees grow from them, not babies." Julie took the pips from her as she spoke.

Jenny sat down beside them. "So where can I get some baby seeds from then?" Jenny asked with a sad face.

"Come on Julie. Where do you get baby seeds from?" Angie asked, putting Julie in an awkward position.

"I don't know what to say. Can you tell her Angie?" Julie was turning the tide.

"Yes, go on Angie; tell me, because I want to get some."

Angie thought for a moment. "Cart was right; babies do grow from seeds, but they only grow in people that God chooses. So you can't buy seeds; it's all down to whom God chooses."

Jenny got up. "I hope he chooses me. I must go and tell George," she said.

"Hang on; the rest of your apple is still here!" Julie shouted.

Jenny turned and shouted back, "I don't want it now!"

Julie turned to Angie. "Thanks for that," she said. "Now let's go for our walk."

As they made their way up the lane, Angie asked what she would do if Jenny did become pregnant.

"I don't think I need to worry about that," Julie replied.

"I hope not, but I think you should talk to her properly about it. She and George are quite close." Angie was truly concerned.

"I know, but I don't think it would ever lead to anything sexual. I have thought about it, but I'm afraid if I tell her what it's about, it might teach them something they would have never known."

"I know what you're saying; it is quite difficult. I'm glad it's a decision I haven't got to make."

The two of them called for Sarah on their way up to Julie's meadow. Julie had a pocket full of candles when they got there, and they sat in their usual place beside the pool. Angie told them that Andrew had told the bishop about his feelings for her.

"What did the bishop say?" Sarah asked.

"He wished him good luck."

"So what's the plan for the future then?" Julie asked.

"I hope we can get married and spend the rest of our lives together. I just love him to bits," Angie said. It was as if she wanted the world to know.

The three of them laughed and joked like three young teenagers until Angie started to think about her past again.

"Do you think God will forgive me for what I have done in my life?" she asked with a sad face.

"Forgive you," Julie said quite forcefully. "What the hell has he got to forgive you for? You have done nothing to forgive. I don't know how Andrew's God would see it, but my God would be proud of you for staying alive."

"There are things I'm ashamed of that I haven't told anyone." Angie had tears in her eyes.

"Nothing can be so bad that you should carry a burden on your shoulders," Julie said, trying to comfort her.

"You think so - what if I told you I planned to kill two people? What would you think of me then?"

"Did you?" Sarah asked, with a bit of a gasp.

"No - but only because I was stopped. The first was my father; I knew he was going to come to my room, so I took the carving knife from the kitchen drawer and put it under my pillow. When he came to get in my bed, I pulled out the knife and tried to stab him, but he grabbed my arm and took the knife off me."

"You poor thing. What happened then?" Julie asked, as she put her arm around her.

"He hit me hard across the face and told me I was ungrateful."

"Well, I know you're forgiven for that one. I think anyone would have killed the bastard."

"The other was the man that ran that awful house. One night there was a repulsive Russian man; he was a crew member on a ship at Millbay Docks. He was covered in some sort of skin condition, so I refused to go with him. The man lifted Amy up by her hair and held her out over the landing. He said he would drop her unless I agreed, so I did. Later that night when everyone was gone to bed, I went to his room, again with a knife. As I went to stab him, I noticed just in time that he wasn't in the bed. It was one of the girls; he had gone to one of the other girl's rooms. I could have killed her. How would I have lived with that?"

"You are too good. If I didn't know better, I would say you and Julie were sisters. You should think no more about it, and get on with your life," Sarah said, as she looked at her watch.

"Amy seems to be enjoying herself here with us all," Julie said.

"I know, I can't believe it; she had a lot of books to look at that showed her animals and the countryside, but until we came here, she had never been outside, and now it's like she has always known it."

Sarah looked at her watch again. "We have to go know; I have the nurse coming for my check-up."

"We better get going then; hadn't better be late for that," Julie said with a big smile.

The three of them lit some candles and started to walk back to the farm. As they went through the bottom of the next field, Julie noticed a bus up in the gateway at the top of the field. "Do you think he is trying to turn around?" she asked.

"I expect so; it's too narrow to get any further up the lane. We have asked the council to put up a sign," Sarah said.

"Perhaps they will know that Arnold is no longer on the council," Julie replied with a large grin.

As they approached the yard, there seemed to be another bus turning up the lane. "I better find John and get him to go up the lane to see if they need a hand," Sarah said with some concern.

John was in the barn when Sarah shouted to him. He came down the steps just as the nurse drove in the yard. She got out of her car and said there was some commotion down at the village. "Loads of old vans and buses - it was a job to get through."

Sarah told John about the bus at the top of the field and the one that had tuned up the lane. John left and went up the lane. Angie and Julie went home, and Sarah went indoors with the nurse. The nurse had nearly finished when George and Jenny came in full of excitement. "We have just seen a van all painted with flowers," George said, as the pair of them sat down at the table. Both were panting.

Sarah poured them both a glass of squash and continued to talk to the nurse.

Jenny suddenly got up and ran down to the lodge. "Mummy, Mummy!" she shouted as she opened the door.

"Whatever is it dear? What's wrong?" Julie asked as she came to the door to meet her.

"Can we have Brussels sprouts for tea?" Jenny asked with her pleading smile.

"Why dear, you don't like them," Julie replied. She put her arm around her and smiled.

"I will eat them; I promise."

"Why? What's brought this on?"

"Well, babies don't grow from seeds, and God doesn't choose people; they are made of iron."

"Whatever makes you think that?" Julie asked, looking rather bewildered.

"Well, I have just been up to Sarah's, and the nurse told her she needs iron to make the baby grow, and the best thing was to eat plenty of sprouts, so if I eat them I might have a baby grow."

"I don't think you got that quite right," Julie said with a smile. "But you can have some sprouts if you like."

Chapter Fourteen

John had gone up the lane, and when he got to the higher field, nothing could have prepared him for what he was confronted with. There were three old buses all covered with paintings of flowers and five or six old vans painted the same way; some had chimneys coming out of the roofs. In the corner, there was an old Ford Zephyr, and the occupants where erecting a tepee tent. John went up to a man who seemed to be the organiser; he was dressed in what John could only describe as some sort of flowery dress.

"What the hell is going on?" John shouted.

"Peace man," the man replied. "Peace," he said again, raising two fingers in the air.

"This is my field, and I want you all to pack up and go now!" John shouted.

By this time, a group had come over and surrounded John, most of them women. The women formed a circle around John and the man in the flowery dress and started to dance around them. "This can't be your field," the man replied. "It's everyone's field; fields belong to the people, man," he said.

"I can show you the deeds; trust me, it's my field, and I want you all to leave."

"Where do you think we should go to?" asked one of the women, who had pushed her way through the dance circle. She was clutching a young child dressed in rags; his face was dirty, and his nose needed to be wiped.

"I suggest you go back to where you come from," John said quite angrily.

"That won't happen," the man replied. "Besides, I think we will like it here."

Two other women came over and started putting their hands all over John. "Love man," they kept saying. John broke away from them, half full of embarrassment and half full of rage.

"You haven't heard the last of this," John said as he stormed off down across the field.

He reached the farm and stormed into the kitchen. "Whatever is the matter?" Sarah asked.

John told her about the hippies moving into the top field.

"It's unlike you to let something like that get to you. I have never seen you like this before; you didn't get like that when Billy Penrose and his family moved in; in fact, you fed them."

"That's different; they were proper Romanies. They were good, honest folks, not like this bunch of no-gooders, who think the world owes them."

"John, John, calm down; you don't know. They might be nice people, and besides they might be gone tomorrow," Sarah said. She put her arm around him.

"I don't think so; they told me the field belonged to everyone, and they were there to stay, and I think you will change your mind about them when you see the state of the kids."

"I haven't formed an opinion to change yet," Sarah said quite sharply.

With that, Cart came into the kitchen, followed by Julie and Fred. Andrew wasn't far behind.

"What's going on?" Cart asked, panting for breath.

"Bloody hippies, that's what," John shouted, "bloody hippies."

"Have you given them permission to be there?" Cart asked.

"No I bloody well haven't. I went up and asked them to leave, and all they did was laugh at me."

"Best you get Sergeant Gibbs out here; he will soon move them on," Cart said angrily.

"I suggest we all calm down and wait until the morning and see what happens," Sarah said, trying to calm the situation. "After all, you might get them out of there and then they end up down on the church green. At least they can't do a great deal of damage where they are."

"You're probably right," John said, as he calmed down. "But I think we should move the cows out that are in the field."

"I'll give you a hand," Fred said.

"I'll come with you." Cart wanted to see what was going on.

"We will have to walk them out the bottom gate and take them through Julie's meadow and over to the next field."

The three of them rounded up the ten or so cows and slowly moved them through Julie's meadow. When they got to the big pool, their eyes almost popped out. There were about twenty naked men, woman and children running in and out of the pool.

When they passed them, trying hard not to look, four of the woman got out of the pool and started to walk beside them. "Bugger off," Cart said, waving his hand.

But the woman kept following. "Peace man," one of the women said, as she got alongside Fred.

Fred quickened his step to get away from the woman. "Do you like what we stand for?" she asked.

"What's that then?" Fred asked angrily as he turned to face her.

"Make love not war, so if you feel like joining us there is plenty of love to go around."

"I have all the love I need, thank you," he replied. "Now if you'll just leave us to get on with our work."

As they stood in front of Cart naked, he said quiet forcefully, "You want that ass of yours slapped?"

One of them turned and put her arms around Cart. "Is that an offer granddad?" she asked.

Cart pushed her hard away. "You aren't doing your kind any favours," he said.

"Oh and what kind is that?" one of the other women asked.

"Bloody scrounging ragamuffins," Cart replied, waving his hands forcefully.

The women turned and ran back to the pool, and the men shifted the cows to the next field and returned to the farm. They went the long way back down around Stoney

Moor so that they wouldn't have to pass the pool again.

When they got back to the farm, Julie was there with Sarah.

"Did you see them again?" Julie asked as they all walked into the kitchen.

Fred told them what had happened. Sarah started to laugh. "Sorry," she said, "but I can just imagine your faces."

"It's not funny," John said angrily. "First thing tomorrow morning, I'm off to see Sergeant Gibbs."

"Come on," Julie said, as she went over and caught hold of Fred's hand. "Let's go home; you never know, they might be gone in the morning."

"I think that's for the best," Sarah agreed. "Let's see what tomorrow brings."

They all agreed and made their way home.

John and Fred could not resist looking up across the field all evening. They could see that the travellers had a large fire burning; this was making John quite mad.

It was just before nine when John was about to go outdoors again. "Come on," Sarah said. "Don't go out again; you know it will only upset you. Now let's have an early night, and we can take a fresh look at it in the morning."

"We can't go to bed yet; George hasn't come up from Julie's," John said, itching to go out again.

"Come on; we will walk down to Julie's and have a coffee; then we can bring George up with us."

When they got down to the lodge, Fred was standing on top of the hedge looking up to the field with the travellers. "What are the buggers doing now?" John asked.

"Can't see, but they got one hell of a fire up there, and the music - how are they playing music?"

"I don't know; they seem to have electric lights up there. I suppose they have some sort of generator."

"Come on you two," Julie shouted. "I have made your coffee."

They went in and had their coffee, and it wasn't long before John, George and Sarah made their way back to the farm and bed.

The next morning, Julie rang Sarah up from the lodge and asked if George could go over to Jan's and get her a couple of dozen eggs. "I haven't any down here for the breakfasts," she said.

"That's fine," Sarah replied, just as George entered the room. She hung up and passed the message on to George. This pleased him, as he could go down early and have his breakfast with Jenny and the visitors.

George soon grabbed his coat and ran off down towards Jan's place. When he got there, he was met at the door by Jan's Mrs. "Hello George, my handsome," she said. "I bet you came for eggs.

"Yes please. Julie will pay later," George replied quite excitedly.

"You better go out back and see Mr; he'll sort you out."

George went through the farm gate at the side of the cottage that led into the fields that they were turning into a traditional farm. A long wall went down the other side of the gate, which separated the farm from the garden where Angie and Amy lived. Standing on a chair looking over the wall was Amy, and on the other side was Cart and Jan, both scratching a sow's back. Amy was laughing, and the pig was grunting.

"You come for your eggs?" Jan asked, as he saw George arrive. "I'll just go and get them. It's a good thing you came now because Mr Creaber's chap is coming over for all we got in a minute."

Jan went into the wooden shed adjoining the back of the cottage. He shouted, "Cart, Mr Creaber hasn't been for his eggs, has he?"

"Not as long as I've been here," Cart replied.

"There's none here; they are all gone, all thirty dozen," Jan said, looking puzzled.

Amy thought all the commotion about the eggs was quite funny because now Cart and Jan were scratching their heads instead of scratching the pig's back. Angie came over to the wall to fetch Amy and to get her off to school. Andrew appeared after walking over from the church. "Is Cart there?" he asked.

"Yes," Angie replied, as her face lit up to see him.

Andrew approached the wall. "Morning," was all he said as he looked down on the three of them on the other side.

"Morning vicar," came the reply.

"Is Olive all right?" Andrew asked in a concerned tone.

"She was when I left; why do you ask?"

"Well, in all the years I have been here, it's the first time she hasn't put the flowers in church on a Wednesday night."

"Oh, she did all right because she had every flower in the garden, and old Percy Symons from the allotment association brought in a big armful."

"Well, there are none there now; come to think of it, the old ones are gone, so she must have been there."

"George you better get back to Julie. I have a dozen eggs indoors; you better take some with you," Angie said.

"If you come over to the vicarage, I have a dozen as well; that should get her through breakfast."

"Cart said I better go and see Olive about her flowers. I may go over and see what time John is going to Tavy. I might go with him."

"I think you should," Angie said, as she returned with the eggs and handed them to George.

George ran over to the vicarage and got the dozen eggs from Andrew and then ran all the way to the lodge. He was full of excitement. He couldn't wait to tell everyone about the vanishing eggs.

Cart left and went to see Olive about the missing flowers. This upset her immensely, as it was the most flowers she had put there for a long time. "The last time there was so many flowers there was when it was Julie's wedding," she said.

Chapter Fifteen

Cart went over to the farm after telling Olive about the flowers. He was met by John and Sarah out in the yard. "Still got your visitors?" he asked, looking up across the fields to where the travellers were.

"Afraid so," John replied. "I'm going in Tavy now to see Sergeant Gibbs. I thought they might be going; I couldn't sleep last night wondering what they were up to, and one of the vans went out about two o'clock this morning, but I see he was back up there just now."

"That's why I've come over; I thought I might give you a bit of support," Cart said, as he went on to tell them about the eggs and the flowers. "I bet those buggers had them," he said as he scratched his head.

"Eggs maybe, but I don't think they would go in church and take the flowers. What purpose could they possibly have in doing that?" Sarah asked calmly.

"I don't know, but I wouldn't trust them, especially that bugger with a skirt on. What man would wear a skirt?" Cart asked with a look of bewilderment.

"Do you think we should go up and ask them about the eggs and flowers?" John asked. He too was quite calm under the circumstances.

"No darling, leave it to the police. Just go in and report it, and let them deal with it," Sarah said as she leaned up and kissed him.

"Come on then Cart, let's go in and see the Sergeant." As they left the yard, a van sped past the yard entrance. "I bet he isn't even taxed," Cart said, as the van narrowly missed the front of the car.

They went in and told Sergeant Gibbs all about the travellers and about the eggs and flowers.

"I'll get Roberts to get right over there now, but we won't be able to move them on; that's a civil matter."

"How do you mean a civil matter?" John asked.

"What I say - you would have to go to court to get them evicted, before we got involved."

"That's outrageous," John said quite angrily. "They are trespassing on my land."

"I know, but trespass is not a criminal offence; it is a civil offence, which is decided in a court of law. Now if they have stolen things, that becomes a different thing altogether. I will investigate that, and if I think they're guilty, trust me I will make their life hell. I'll get Adams up their now and I'll come over this afternoon. Trust me; I will do all I can within my powers to help."

"Thanks for that," John said, as they turned and left the police station. "Just as well leave the car here a minute," John said. "I want to walk over to the ironmongers and get some padlocks."

"Sorry day when you got to lock things up in a village like ours," Cart replied.

As they walked across the square, there was the van that nearly hit them parked. Laid out on the pavement behind it were eggs, bunches of flowers, potatoes and vegetables, and in the middle of them was a girl no more than nine or ten selling them.

Cart and John went over to her. "Where's the driver of the van?" John asked, kneeling down beside her.

"I don't know," came the reply.

The girl looked dirty; her dress was all ripped, and her hair was down past her shoulders and looked like it had never been brushed.

"I think some of this stuff has been stolen," John said, still kneeling down beside her.

"I don't know," the girl replied. "Now you should go; you are putting off the customers, and Spud won't be very happy."

"Spud won't be very happy when the police get here," Cart said sharply, which scared the girl.

"Don't frighten her," John said, feeling quite sorry for the girl. "It's not her fault."

"I know; it just makes me mad to see a child like this. The parents should be locked up. We should go back and tell the Sergeant, don't you think?" Cart said.

"Yes, then let's get back to the farm."

As they returned to Tremarrow, the Sergeant went over to the girl selling things in the square. "Where did you get these things?" he asked.

"Why?" came a voice from behind the parked van.

"Why? Because I need to know if they are stolen," the Sergeant replied.

"How can they be? They are all a gift from nature," said the man, who came around from the back of the van.

"That may be, but they still belong to someone, so I will ask again. Where did they come from?" The Sergeant looked quite stern.

"Out of the back of my van," came the reply.

"I believe them to be stolen," the Sergeant said, as he turned his attention to the van. "You aren't displaying a tax disc."

"Don't know where that's gone," the man replied.

"Have you got insurance?"

"I think so; it's not my van."

"Then whose is it?"

"Everyone's."

"How do you mean everyone's? Who is everyone?" The Sergeant was now getting quite angry. He was beginning to think the man was taking him for a fool. "What's your name?" he asked.

"Spud."

"No, your full name," the Sergeant said, as he took a notebook out of his pocket.

"That is my name. That's what I am known as."

The man and Sergeant Gibbs had now moved to the front of the van. The little girl was doing a roaring trade despite the presence of the Sergeant.

"Now I need your real name and address, or I will arrest you," the Sergeant said as he licked the end of his pencil.

"My address is the van, wherever it might be, and I have already told you my name."

"Is the little girl your daughter?" the Sergeant asked.

"Who knows the answer to that one," the man replied.

"Look, I'm losing my patience with you; now tell me, is she your daughter?"

"As I said, who knows? She might be. I treat her as my daughter; she lives with me and her mother, but I can't be sure I'm her father."

"Right, I know where you are staying. I need you to pack up now, and I will be over presently, and I need answers on where these items came from. I also need to see the documents regarding your van and a driving licence."

The Sergeant left the man and went back to the police station.

Back at Tremarrow, John, Cart, Sarah and Julie were joined by Olive and Fred. They were all sitting around the kitchen table drinking coffee and discussing the travellers. When there was a knock at the door, Sarah went and answered it. Gilbert Lane stood there, his cap on one side of his head, which he removed. "Tell your husband to get those bloody people off his land," he said.

"Come in Gilbert," John shouted. Gilbert walked into the kitchen. "Now, what seems to be the problem?" John asked.

"Tiddies, that's the problem. I put out ten bags of tiddies on the milk stand last night for Sammy to pick up for market today. But when he got there, they were gone, and we all know where, don't we?"

Sarah and Julie looked at each other and smiled almost to laughter; it always cracked them up when Gilbert said *tiddies*.

"Well, I have seen Sergeant Adams, so you best tell him," John said, as he showed him to the door quite quickly because he knew Olive didn't like it when he was around.

Sarah and John's farm always had an open door, and it wasn't long before Percy Symons arrived at the door. He explained how a lot of his vegetables had been taken from the allotments. He also brought a copy of the morning news with him, which made interesting reading.

The story read:

TRAVELLERS TURN ON THEIR OWN

A large community of new age travellers and CND followers, who are camped on the outskirts of Plymouth, yesterday evicted about twenty or so travellers from their site.

I spoke to the leader of the camp, who told me that the group that they moved on had entirely different views than theirs and CND. They are led by a man who calls himself "Viceroy" (ruler of a colony).

The group was made to leave after a spate of petty thefts that happened after their arrival; it would appear that the group had no apparent respect for people's property or positions. The man also said that the police seem to have very little power to deal with them, so the group decided to remove them from their site.

"What now then?" Cart asked, as John finished reading the paper.

"I don't know," John replied. "If it was just the men, I would suggest we throw them off with force if necessary, but the problem is the children. That girl in Tavistock this morning brought tears to my eyes."

"I suggest we wait until the police have seen them, and if they are still there, then we ask them down for a meeting," Julie said, as she helped Sarah pass around more coffee.

"That's probably best," Olive said in agreement.

"If we do hold a meeting with them, I suggest you ask Mr Knight to attend," Fred said.

"I think that's a good idea," John replied.

Sergeant Gibbs had arrived at the camp only to find two of the women had PC Adams cornered in one of the buses, taunting him with their bodies. It didn't look to Sergeant Adam's as if he was trying very hard to get away.

"What the hell is going on?" the Sergeant shouted.

"I'm under attack," Adams shouted, as he tucked his shirt back into his trousers.

"I want to see the man that calls himself Viceroy," Sergeant Gibbs said firmly.

"That would be me," a man said as he entered the bus. "How can I help you officer?"

"I need to talk to you about selling stolen goods and vehicles with no tax or insurance."

"Really? And what goods might that be?"

"The goods that a young girl was selling in Tavistock this morning."

"Young girl eh? So how does that involve me?"

"Well, was she selling the goods on your say so?"

"On my say so - whatever gives you that idea? You never know what these youngsters get up to," the man said, as the two girls at the back of the bus came forward and put their arms around the man, who kissed them both.

"Perhaps you could show me the documents for this vehicle then," the Sergeant said.

"And why would you want them? As I understand, the law says you only need tax and insurance if the vehicle is on the road. As I see it, we aren't on the road." The man again kissed both women, this time making a point of putting his tongue in their mouths.

"The vehicle was driven here," the Sergeant said, trying not to look at what was going on, which was obviously done to distract him.

"Prove it," the man said. "Now, if you have no further questions, I have other things on my mind." His hand went up under one of the girl's tops, exposing her breasts.

"Don't think this is the end of the matter," the Sergeant said, as he got off the bus and went looking for the van driver.

The young girl that was in town selling the goods was over by the hedge with another little girl, who was about four or five. "Where is your dad?" the Sergeant asked.

"Mummy, Mummy!" the girl shouted, and they both ran over to a shabby looking caravan.

A woman in her late twenties appeared at the door. She was wearing a low-cut bra and a pair of tight short shorts, which had the front button undone and the zipper halfway down, leaving the top gaping open.

"I wonder if I could have a word with your husband," the Sergeant said.

"You'll have a job," the women said as she lit a cigarette.

"And why's that?"

"I haven't got one," came the reply. "I'm no one's possession," the woman replied, as she drew on the cigarette and blew the smoke at the Sergeant.

"Well, can you tell me where I can find the driver of that van?" the Sergeant asked, pointing to a van parked by the hedge where the young girls were.

"I don't know; haven't seen him for ages. Would you like to come in and wait?" the woman asked, as she leaned on the door frame, with her breasts only inches away from the Sergeant's face.

"No, but you can give him a message from me. He might think he's clever, but I promise you he won't get away with things with me."

"I'll pass it on; now, is there anything I can do for you?" the woman asked, as she put her hand on his shoulder, lifted her head and smiled.

"No thank you," the Sergeant replied, as he turned and looked around the site, trying to gauge how many people were there.

He left the site and made his way down to the farm to see John. When he got there, Sarah and Julie where still making coffee, and Cart and Olive were still there. Fred had to go back to his visitors. "Funny lot they are," he said, as John showed him into the kitchen.

"Well, what's happening - are they going to move on?" Cart asked.

"Doesn't look very promising," came an unwanted reply.

"What about the stuff they stole?" John asked.

"We know they stole it, but how do we prove it?"

"Well, me and Cart saw them selling it; surely that's enough," John said, as he sipped at yet another cup of coffee.

"I know it was your stuff she was selling, but can you prove it or who stole it? The only thing I could do, if you could prove it was yours, is arrest a young girl as she was selling it. But how do you prove who stole it?"

"I think we will have to go with Fred's idea, and try and hold a meeting with them," John said.

"How many are there up there do you think?" Julie asked.

"I'm not sure. I saw five children, and there were six men I saw, but I know there is another one somewhere. I counted fourteen women between about eighteen and thirty."

"I saw more of them yesterday than I wanted to," Cart said, which brought a smile from Sarah and Julie.

"If you want me to come along to your meeting, just let me know; I'll be going up there every day to try and put pressure on them," the Sergeant said as he left.

The Sergeant had just left when Angie came in. "Are we still going for our walk?" she asked as she entered the kitchen.

"Why not?" Sarah said, as she stood up. "It's our property, and no one is stopping me from walking on our ground."

"Good for you," Julie replied. "Let's go."

"You forgot lunch," John said with a smile.

"Oh sorry. With all the goings on, I never thought about it."

"Don't you worry," Olive said. "I'll knock John up a sandwich; you go on for your walk."

"Thanks," they said, as they left and made their way across the yard.

The three of them walked up across the fields to Julie's meadow as they did most days. As they approached the meadow, they could see people in the distance around the large pool. "I hope they respect this place," Julie said, as they made their way across the meadow.

There were what looked to be four young girls ranging from about four to eight playing in the water. "At least the children look happy," Sarah said with a little smile.

Beside the pool sitting on the grass were two women in their late twenties, each dressed in a white dress. One of them stood up as the three of them approached. She stood with the sun behind her; you could see right through the thin white cotton dress. It was obvious that she had nothing on underneath. Angie stopped, looking startled. "Sally?" she said, sounding surprised.

"Angie," the woman replied, also quite startled. "What are you doing here?"

"I live here. More to the point, what are you doing here?" Angie asked, still looking quite bewildered.

"You know this lady?" Julie asked, sounding as surprised as Angie.

"Yes, she was in the same place as me; only she wasn't a prisoner. She could come and go as she liked," Angie said angrily.

"It was your own fault you were a prisoner, as you call it," Sally said. "You should never have been so rebellious. I think you thought your body was some sort of temple. If it wasn't for you, we could still be living there now."

"I don't think of my body as a temple, but it's my body, and I should decide what I do with it, not some uncouth man," Angie said angrily.

Sally laughed at her. "Who do you think you are, you self-righteous little shit? You made us homeless with your high bloody morals."

"How can you say that?" Julie said angrily. "Angie is a human being who has been abused all her life; I admire her for her morals, and yes, it's a good thing that place is closed down."

"What do you know about it? You're just a country bumpkin who's never been in the real world. I don't suppose you ever had a real man," Sally said, as she eyed Julie up and down.

"If I'm a country bumpkin, then I'm proud of it. It's the way I want to stay because I don't believe there's a better life anywhere. Oh, and yes, I have a real man, far more of a man than one who abuses women. Yes, he treats my body like a temple as I do his."

"You want to get yourself in the real world, love. Why do you think God gave us our bodies? For us to use for survival, that's what," Sally said, as she still eyed Julie up and down.

"All I can say is I feel sorry for you; God gave us our bodies to give to the one we love, and as far as I'm concerned, the love I give and get back far outweighs anything in this world," Julie replied, with her face glowing with contentment.

"How did you get involved with these people?" Angie asked.

"When we got kicked out of the big house, those of us that wouldn't make statements just got left with nowhere to go, so I walked into their camp and met Viceroy. He said I could become one of his women. I thought it better than walking the streets."

"You mean he has more than one woman?" Julie asked quite abruptly.

"Yes, I think there are about seven of us," Sally replied.

"What? You all make love with him?" Julie couldn't believe what she was hearing.

"Not all at the same time," Sally replied, "although three of us did one night, but usually it's just one or two."

"How awful," Julie replied, as she screwed up her nose.

"You ought to try it one night before you dismiss it; you might surprise yourself and enjoy it." Sally laughed at her whilst she spoke.

"Come on," Sarah said. "This is making me feel quite sick. I want to go back now."

The three of them left and made their way back to the farm.

Chapter Sixteen

Two days had passed, and although a meeting could not be arranged away from the camp, it had been decided that a number of villagers, Sergeant Gibbs and Mr Knight would go to the camp and confront them. Mr Knight arrived at the farm quite early, as he wanted to discuss the options Sarah and John had, which to be honest weren't a lot.

"Have you any more news on Rupert?" Sarah asked him, as they all sat around the kitchen table.

"Nothing - it will probably take months of legal arguments. I know they have charged Lenard James with perjury and I think they will wait for the outcome of his case before there is a decision made on Rupert."

Other villagers arrived along with Sergeant Gibbs. They all congregated out in the yard before making their way up to the camp. PC Adams was not there, as the Sergeant had decided he was going to have him keep a watch on them at night to see if he could catch them red-handed nicking things.

They all made their way up the lane. As they entered the camp, they were met by a group of men and women. The one they call Viceroy was not visible.

"We want to speak to whoever is in charge," John said, in a voice that sounded as if he meant business.

"I don't know if he is available," came the reply from one of the men.

"Well, I think he should make himself available, and pretty dam pronto," came a reply from the Sergeant.

With that, Viceroy appeared, flanked by two women. "What's all the commotion?" he asked in a soft voice.

"We want to know when you are leaving!" shouted Percy Symons. "You have wrecked our gardens."

"And when are you paying me for my bloody tiddies you stole?" Gilbert Lane shouted.

"Whoa, whoa," the Viceroy intervened. "Let's have a little bit of order. We don't shout, do we? We treat people with respect."

"That's good, coming from you," John said. "You have no respect for our property or our possessions," John said angrily.

"Just calm down man. Now tell me what these possessions are," the Viceroy said very calmly.

"My tiddies!" Gilbert shouted.

"Our eggs," said Jan.

"My vegetables," Percy said.

"And what about the flowers from the church?" Olive said, as she waved her finger at the man.

"All these things belong to nature, not you; God put them on this earth for everyone. How can you say they are yours?" the Viceroy still spoke in a very quiet voice.

"Of course they're ours. Who do you think planted the seed on my allotment to make them grow?" Percy said.

"You might have put them there on the people's land,

but God made them grow, not you. So therefore they belong to everyone."

"You can't possibly believe that," the Sergeant replied. "Anyhow, what about Jan's eggs?"

"How can they be Jan's eggs, when chickens laid them? The eggs belong to the chickens, if anybody."

"That may be so," Jan said angrily, "but the chicken belongs to me."

"How can you possibly believe that someone can own an animal? They are creatures of God, just like us humans; no one can own us."

"You don't half-talk a load of claptrap," Cart said. "You need to get off John's land, and let us get on with our lives."

"It's our land, the people's land - no one can own land. Yes, hundreds of years ago, people put up fences and tried to claim it, but who said they could? I don't believe God did."

Andrew had been quiet until now. "Let me ask you. Do you really believe in God, or are you trying to hide behind him to justify yourself?"

"Oh, a smart vicar," the Viceroy replied. "Perhaps you should look at things the way we all do here, before you make your mind up on who's right and who's wrong."

"I don't need to look any further. I have seen enough - stealing, trespassing, no respect for other people, treating women as sex objects, exploiting children. My world might not be perfect, but I know which one is right."

"Hear hear!" came a shout from the villagers.

Mr Knight stepped forward and told the man who he was, before continuing. "We have all come here today to try and come to an amicable conclusion, but it is obvious that you are not prepared to listen. My clients are prepared to give you forty-eight hours to remove all vehicles and yourselves from their land; failing to do so will leave them no alternative than to apply to the high court for a writ to have you physically removed."

"Good luck with that mate; we are going nowhere. It might surprise you what rights we have."

The visitors, all disenchanted, left and made their way back to the village.

That night, PC Adams arrived with the police minivan. He parked about twenty yards up the road from the gateway; he arrived about eight o'clock, not in police uniform - he was excited to think that he was on an undercover mission. After about two hours, he was getting quite bored and stiff, so he decided to get out and have a look in the gateway. He hadn't realised that the travellers had seen him arrive in his van.

As he crept in around the gateway, he was startled by two of the women. "Hello," one of them said. "Do you want to look around our camp?"

"I'd love to," he replied, not realising they knew who he was. He thought it would be a good chance to have a real good snoop around; the Sarge will be pleased with me, he thought.

The women led him around the camp, showing him where everyone lived. As they came back around the site towards the gate, they led him into the tepee tent. It was lit with a row of candles at the far end; on the floor was a large mattress. "Sit down," one of the women said. She sat down on the mattress, pulling the PC down as she did.

"Do you know what this place is?" the other woman said, as she sat down on the other side of him, getting very close.

"No," the PC said, as he gulped with nervousness.

"This is the love tent," said the woman who had sat down first. She put her arm around his neck.

"Oh, really, I must go now," the PC said, as he started to get up.

"Don't go yet," the other woman said. She put her hand on his shoulder, pushing him back down.

"You can't leave us," the other woman said, as she ran her fingers through his hair.

The PC gulped and pulled the woman's hand down.

"What's wrong? Don't you like us?" the women said in a sad tone.

"Yes, I like you."

"Then what's wrong?" the woman asked, as she unbuttoned his shirt.

"I really do have to be going," the PC said, pulling the woman's hand away from his shirt buttons.

"Your wife won't know," the other woman said.

"I'm not married," the PC replied.

"Well, girlfriend then."

"I don't have a girlfriend," the PC replied, his voice quivering.

"Then you don't have to rush, do you?" the woman said. She took his hand and held it against her breast.

"Does that feel nice?" the other woman asked, as she took his other hand and placed it on her breast.

"Yes," he replied. He had no idea what to do. Should he just get up and run, or should he stay and see what happens? It was the first time he had ever touched a woman, let alone two.

"Would you like to see what you are touching?" one of the women asked.

"I don't know - I do have to go - I've got work to do," the PC said, as he removed his hand from her breast.

"Oh, and what work is that then?" both women asked together.

"I can't say; its top secret," the PC replied. He again tried to get up.

"You aren't going anywhere," one of the woman said quite crossly. "You do what I say, or I will tell everyone what you have done to us."

"I haven't done anything," the PC said, looking quite innocent.

"Who do you think will believe you," one of the women said, "when the two of us tell them you had kinky sex with us?"

"You wouldn't do that; why would you?" The PC was now in a very difficult situation.

"We will, if you don't do what we say. Now you should just as well lie back and enjoy it," the woman said, as she pushed him back on the mattress.

The other woman removed her dress to reveal her naked body. She put a leg on each side of the PC and sat on him. "Do you like what you see?" she asked, as she unfastened the rest of his shirt buttons.

The other woman took of his shoes, as the PC brought his hands up and started to fondle the naked woman's body. "Not yet," she said, as she lifted his hand from her body.

The naked woman then got up, and the other woman moved up between his legs and started to undo his trousers. "Let's see if you are a big boy," she said, as she quite roughly pulled off his pants.

The woman who was naked disappeared out of the tent whilst the other woman removed PC's clothes. He was naked, except for his socks.

The other woman returned with a rolled-up cigarette in her mouth. She sat down beside the PC, took the cigarette out of her mouth and held it up to him. Suddenly, there was a flash from the opening in the tent. The PC jumped up and looked to see Viceroy standing in the tent opening. He had a camera in his hand.

"What the hell?" he said, trying to find something to cover his modesty to no avail, as the other woman had left the tent with his clothes.

"I think it's time for you to leave," Viceroy said in a quiet voice.

"What are you going to do with that camera?" the PC asked abruptly.

"That all depends on you now. I suggest you clear off before the owl comes out and eats that little worm," Viceroy said, as he turned to go out of the tent.

"What about my clothes?" the PC asked.

"Sorry, you aren't having them. You should have been a good boy, shouldn't you have?" the Viceroy said. He and the women left, leaving the PC in the tent.

With all the carrying on, PC Adams hadn't noticed that one of the vans had gone out. As he gingerly made his way back to the minivan, he searched the van for something to cover his modesty, but there was nothing there.

Suddenly, the radio in the van was going. "Sergeant Gibbs to Adams, come in," the voice said three times.

He picked up the receiver. "Adams here," he replied.

The rest of the conversation went like this:

"Where have you been? I have been trying to contact you, over."

"Been checking something out, over."

"Get your ass down to John and Sarah's and block off the lane to the lodge, over."

"I can't at the moment, over."

"Why not? Over."

"I have a small problem, over."

"I don't care what your problem is; you get down there. Someone is stealing sheep, over."

"I'm on my way, over."

PC Adams went back into the camp to see if he could get his clothes back or find something to cover himself with, but to no avail. He went back to the minivan, drove down to the farm and parked across the top of the lane. He had only just stopped when Sarah and Julie approached the van. "John and Fred have gone up towards Stone moor to make sure they don't try to get away across the fields," Sarah said as she approached the van.

"Aren't you cold without a shirt on?" Julie said, as she too approached the van window.

"No. I'm all right." Then he suddenly shouted, "Don't come any closer."

"Why not? We aren't the enemy. I think you should stand over by the wall. You can look right down the lane, and you can see their torchlight," Julie said as she opened the van door.

Looking away from the van towards the wall as she opened the door, Julie suddenly heard Sarah's shriek. "Look!"

Julie turned to see PC Adams naked. She just roared with laughter.

"I can explain," Adams said. He was franticly pulling the door shut.

"I hope you can," Sarah said as she tried to hold back the laughter.

Suddenly, car lights appeared, as Sergeant Gibbs came roaring into the yard. He got out of his car and approached Sarah and Julie.

"I'll take Adams with me and see if I can catch them in the act," he said.

"I'll just go in and find him something to wear," Sarah said, walking over towards her back door.

"How do you mean?" the Sergeant asked as he looked towards the van. "Adams, get over here now!" he shouted in a voice that no one would disobey. Adams got out of the van, his hands modestly covering his private parts. The Sergeant then shouted, "Adams, get back in the van!" Adams jumped back in the van. Julie could not control her laughter.

Sarah soon returned with a pair of trousers and one of John's shirts.

"I hope you got a bloody good explanation," the Sergeant said, as he took the clothes from Sarah and handed them to Adams.

Suddenly, there where lights coming up the lane. Then they unexpectedly stopped. The Sergeant and Adams (now dressed) stood in front of the van waiting for the travellers' van to arrive. As it approached them, the Sergeant held his hand up for it to stop. It came to a halt about six feet in front of them.

"What's wrong?" the driver asked, trying to look surprised to see them.

"Do you mind if I look in the back of your van?" the Sergeant asked.

"Help yourself," the man replied.

The Sergeant and Adams went to the back of the van and opened the door, only to find the van empty. They hadn't realised that when the lights had stopped in the lane, it was because the man had seen them and had let the lambs out of the back.

The Sergeant slammed the door shut, with his temper showing. "This is your bloody fault," he said to Adams.

"Is there a problem?" the van driver asked. "I got lost, and then I got stuck turning around."

"I thought I said this vehicle was not to go on the road until it had tax and insurance," the Sergeant said, still mad as hell that they hadn't caught him rustling.

The driver, Spud, asked the Sergeant if he would move the minivan so that he could get out.

"There's only one place where you are going - to the

station with me. I have asked you for your name, and you refused. It is apparent that this vehicle is neither taxed nor insured," the Sergeant said. He put a set of handcuffs on Spud, put him in the back of his car and returned to the van, which he started to search.

John and Fred came walking up the lane. "No lambs in the van," PC Adams shouted to them.

"I know that; he let them out halfway up the lane when he saw you," John replied.

"I found something - might help find out who he is," the Sergeant said. He got out of the van, waving a logbook in his hand.

John was looking at PC Adams. "If I didn't know better, I would say you got my shirt and trousers on," he said.

"I have," he said quietly, his face going red with embarrassment.

"Why is that then?" John asked.

"Sarah will explain." He got in and reversed Spud's van back out of the way.

The Sergeant parked the van in the corner of John's yard, locked it up, put police tape around it and took Spud off to Tavistock police station, where he placed him in a cell for the night. "You report to me nine o'clock sharp," he said to Adams as he left. Adams followed the Sergeant out of the yard.

Chapter Seventeen

The next morning, after interviewing Spud and showing him the logbook, it was obvious that the Sergeant was getting nowhere. So he phoned the directory enquires service to see if he could get a phone number for the name in the logbook. The address was a village in Hampshire; the operator gave him a number, which he phoned. "Good morning sir; did you own a J4 van?" he asked.

"Did about twelve months ago," came the reply. "Why do you ask?"

The Sergeant explained who he was, and then asked if he could remember the person he sold it to.

"Spud," the man replied.

"Spud - Who is Spud?"

"Oh sorry, that's how we knew him; he always had potatoes for sale, but no one knew where he got them from. His real name is Joe Swale."

"Can you tell me anything else about him?"

"You ought to ask your mates up here; they were always interviewing him about petty thefts. He left here with Bill Thomas and his Bedford bus."

"Is there anything you can tell me about him?"

"Once again, you should ask your mates up here; Bill

Thomas was charged with having sex with an underage girl, but as far as I know, the case collapsed. The girl concerned withdrew her allegation. Do you know where he is? I would like to contact him."

"I might know. Can you tell me why you would want to contact him?"

The phone went quiet for a while. Then the man said Bill had a lot of women. "He always said that God had told him that love was for sharing. Whether he believed it or not, I'm not sure. As time went on he started to convince women - even quite intelligent women - that God would enter them through him. Later, he started nicking things, saying God told him everything belonged to everyone and no one owned anything. He built himself up as some kind of cult figure and got booted out of the village."

"I don't understand why you want to find him," the Sergeant said.

"It's my friend Sam. When the villagers booted Bill out of the village, he took Sam's wife and daughter with him. In fact, there were about five women who left their homes and went with him. Sam couldn't care less about his wife, but he worries about his daughter. He would just like her to contact him."

"How old would she be and what are their names?" the Sergeant asked.

"Sally Jiles and his daughter Diane - she's got to be nearly sixteen now, I should think."

"Look, I think the man you call Bill is here, but I have seen no one around fifteen or sixteen with them. But I will make inquiries and will contact you with what I find out," the Sergeant said. He then thanked him for his help.

The Sergeant didn't let on to Spud that he now knew who he was, because once he knew his name, he would have to let him go. He decided to phone the police in Hampshire, and what they told him was quite disturbing. He decided to go over to Tremarrow and tell some of the villagers what he had found out. He had grave concerns about the fifteen-year-old girl who might be there.

When he arrived at Tremarrow, he went to the farm. This always was a gathering point for a number of villagers, and sure enough the large kitchen was full. Cart, Olive, Fred, Julie, Andrew and Angie were there. Little Amy was out in the yard with George and Jenny. Sarah was making coffee, and John was taking his boots off outside the door. John saw the Sergeant arrive. "Come on in," he said as he opened the door.

"What? Did you smell the coffee?" Sarah asked, as she reached up and took another cup out of the cupboard.

"Very good; two sugars please," the Sergeant replied, as he sat down around the table with the others.

"What have you got to tell us then?" Cart asked.

"I still got Spud locked up, but I'm a little concerned about a fifteen-year-old girl. Have any of you seen one up there?"

"Why? What's wrong?" Julie asked, sounding concerned.

"I know who the man that calls himself Viceroy is; he has a lot of women following him, and if that's what they want to do, that's up to them. But one of the women who came away with him left her husband and brought her daughter with her. Her husband is worried sick about his daughter."

"You say you are concerned," Julie said. "Can I ask why?"

"Viceroy, as he calls himself, was a school bus driver. There were a number of underage girls who allegedly had sex with him. He was charged with one offence of having sex with a juvenile. The case collapsed when the girl's father stopped her from giving evidence."

"What, you think he might do it with the girl if she is up there?" Sarah was also concerned.

"I think she would be pretty safe with her mother there," Olive said.

"Don't you believe it; he gets these women to do what he wants. They think he's some sort of god," the Sergeant replied.

"Needs his bloody balls cut off if you ask me," Cart chipped in.

"That would be a bit drastic," Andrew replied.

"I don't know. I'm with you Cart," Fred said quite angrily.

"Look, I don't want him to know that I know his name for now, but I do need to know if that girl is up there," the Sergeant said. He put his coffee cup back on the table.

"I tell you what," Julie said, "I will walk up the meadow. Some of the young children are bound to be there; they might tell me."

"I'll go with you," Angie said.

"And me," Sarah said.

"Just try not to make it look like you are asking questions; just take it casual like," the Sergeant said.

"Leave it to us," Julie replied. "We'll suss the situation out."

Sarah was picking up the cups. "You three go on," Olive said. "I'll do your dishes."

"Thanks, John will give you a hand," Sarah replied with a smile.

"I'm not sure how to do that," John replied as the three girls went out the door.

The three of them made their way up through the fields to Julie's meadow. As they thought, some of the women and the children were over by the pool. They went over and sat down on the grass as they normally would. The children were running in and out of the water. The girls decided to let them play and then to gradually speak to them. Much to their surprise, they were soon joined by Viceroy, who had seen them walk across the field.

"Good afternoon, ladies," he said as he approached.

"Good afternoon," they replied together, each with a girly giggle.

"I haven't seen such an array of beauty in a long time," Viceroy said as he sat down beside them.

"Bit of a charmer, aren't you," Angie replied.

"I don't see myself that way; I just say things the way God tells me to."

"Oh, I don't think God would tell you to act in the way you do," Julie said quite angrily.

"Bless you my friend; you are so naive. God entered me one night. He told me that every woman I entered would become the daughter of God."

"I bet he didn't enter you in the same way you are entering them," Angie said quite angrily.

"You are just using women for your own pleasure," Sarah said.

"My dear child, I get no pleasure in what I do. I do it as a duty. Just as a vicar thinks it's his duty to preach in church, it is my duty to let God enter women through me."

"I'll take my chances with the vicar's prayers if it's all the same to you," Sarah said with a smile.

"You may think that now, but you pray tonight when you go to bed, and God's voice will come to you. He will tell you to come to me to be entered, so just remember my bed is always open to you," Viceroy said as he got up.

"Well don't hold your breath, because it doesn't matter how many voices come to me, you won't find me in your bed," Julie said in a forceful way.

"Can you tell me - if God tells you to enter these women and you don't enjoy it - why do you have so many women living with you?" Angie asked.

"They need caring for. I care for them, that's what. I do care for them," he replied.

"Is it God's will to have two women in your bed at the same time? Is that not for your pleasure? Or stripping a police constable naked and not letting him have his clothes - I don't think God would agree to that."

"That's where you are wrong. God said to love one another, as we would want to be loved yourself, and you can't tell me that there isn't one of you who doesn't dream of a pair of you making love with one man."

"I think you got the words wrong. If you go and talk to your god again, I think he will tell you that the word he used was *love*, not lust," Angie said quite firmly.

"And what about the police constable?" Sarah asked. "Do you know how much you embarrassed him?"

"There should be no embarrassment with the human body; we were all born naked and should be proud of our bodies." The Viceroy released his robe and let it drop to the ground; he stood in front of them naked.

Sarah and Julie stood there with red faces, but it didn't embarrass Angie. She had seen it all before, and she knew how to put a man down.

"Of all the men I've seen - and let me tell you I've seen some men in my time - never have I seen such a small one!" Angie said, which caused the other two to giggle.

The Viceroy picked up his robe and scampered up across the meadow, thinking he had met his match. The three of them were finding it all quite funny. "If you thought that was small, you ought to have seen PC Adams," Sarah said, as the tears of laughter ran down her cheek.

It wasn't long before the children who were running in and out of the water sat down on the grass. Julie got up and sat between them. "Hello, I'm Julie; what's your names?"

"I'm Daisy," the little one said.

"Oh that's nice, just like this flower," Julie said, as she picked a daisy and held it up in front of her.

"My name is Bluebell," one of the other children said.

"Oh, we have some of them here as well, but not just at the moment," Julie said. She turned to the girl who was quite a bit older. "And are you called after a flower?" she asked.

"No, I wish I was, I'm called Victoria," she said.

"I think that's nice," Julie said. "Now let me think. I thought you had another friend when you came, someone a bit older than you."

"That's Diane," Daisy said. "She's not allowed out."

"Why, has she been naughty?" Julie whispered.

"I don't know; she has to stay in until after her birthday, so she will be out tomorrow," Victoria said, sounding quite grown up.

Just as she finished her sentence, and before Julie could ask another question, a voice said, "Come on you three; it's time to come up now."

Julie looked behind her at a woman standing there. She had a white dress on and nothing on her feet. She moved over in front of the children, and with the sun behind her, you could see through the cotton dress.

Julie stood up in front of the woman. "I'm Julie."

Sarah and Angie came over and introduced themselves too.

"I'm Sally," the woman replied.

"What lovely children you have," Julie said, hoping to get in on the conversation.

"Oh they aren't mine; they are all Jade's, but she is busy this afternoon."

"Have you any children?" Julie asked, trying to say it in a causal way.

"Just one," the woman said, as she tried to hurry the children up.

Angie thought to try a different approach. "Viceroy has offered me a place in his bed; if I accept, how will the other women react?"

"We will welcome you with open arms; the more love we can bring in the better. When he first enters you, your body will just fill with love. It's God's work you know," Sally said with a glow on her face.

"Perhaps I will come up tonight then," Angie said, trying to sound convincing.

"Oh not tonight," Sally quickly said. "You can't come tonight; we have something on."

"Perhaps tomorrow then," Angie said, as the woman quickly left and hurried up across the meadow.

After she had gone, Julie suddenly turned to the others. She looked like the penny had just dropped. "Do you know what I think?" she said, looking rather nervous.

"What?" the other two shouted.

"The girl they were talking about - I think today is her sixteenth birthday, and that bloody pervert is going to have her tonight. That's why she didn't want you up there," Julie said, as she looked at Angie.

"Do you think so?" Sarah asked. "You don't think you are reading too much into it? After all, Sally's her mother."

"I think you're right," Angie said. "I think we should get back and phone the Sergeant, just to be on the safe side. We could never forgive ourselves if something happened to that girl and we could have stopped it."

The three of them hurried back across the fields to the farm. "You put the kettle on whilst I phone the Sergeant," Sarah said, as the three of them entered the kitchen.

Chapter Eighteen

It was evening when the Sergeant arrived. Angie and Julie had come back over to Sarah's after going home and getting their tea. Amy had gone to spend the night with Cart and Olive. No one had told them what was going on for fear of Cart's reactions.

As they all stood in the farmyard looking up across the fields, they could see candles being lit around the inside of the tepee tent. "There is definitely something happening up there," the Sergeant said.

"What's your plan?" Julie asked.

"I'm not sure. I don't want anything to happen to that girl, but I don't want to just go storming in there."

"What if I went up and pretended I had come to see Viceroy?" Angie suggested.

"I can't put you in danger," the Sergeant said.

"I'll be all right, especially if you are nearby somewhere. I need to do this. I would like to think that after all I've been through, if I help stop one person from being abused, it will make me feel good." Angie looked like she had to do it.

"Okay, but this is what we do; we walk up the lane, not across the fields. You quietly go inside the gate and have a look around; don't say anything to anyone unless you are challenged. If we can find out what's going on without any confrontation, it will be good."

"Well, let's go then," Julie said.

"Hang on. Where do you think you're going?" the Sergeant asked.

"With you of course; you don't think that after all our detective work, we aren't going to be in on the kill?" Julie said laughing.

"All right, but honestly Sarah, I don't think you should come. I can't put you in any danger in your condition."

"The Sergeant's right," John said. "I think you should stay here."

"You're just a spoilsport," Sarah said. Then she paused. "But I know you're right," she said with a smile.

"We'll come for a bit of moral support," Fred said, pointing to John.

Just as they were about to leave to go up the lane, PC Adams arrived on his bike.

"Bloody hell; do I need him for this, or is he going to be a bloody liability?" the Sergeant said as Adams rode his bike into the yard. He got off his bike and walked over to where they were standing.

"Evening Sarge," he said.

"Do you think it's safe for you to go up there?" the Sergeant asked in an angry voice.

"Yes Sarge, you might need me as backup," he replied.

"Tell me. With all the police constables in Devon and Cornwall, why did I have to end up with you?" the Sergeant said. They made their way up the lane.

They got to the field gate and crept in close to the hedge. They were only a few feet away from the back of the tent. With all candles lit inside they could see the silhouettes of people. There was someone lying on the mattress on the floor, with what looked like two women on each side of her. There was the figure of a man naked, standing in front of them.

"Let's get up close to the tent and see if we can hear anything," the Sergeant whispered.

They crept close to the entrance; they could hear what sounded like someone in distress. They could hear whimpering and the same voice: "No Mummy, no - please, Mummy no."

It was clearly apparent what was going on. "Let's get in there and stop it," Julie said quite forcefully.

"Just hang on a minute; try and remember everything that is said." The Sergeant pulled Adams forward as he told him to write everything down.

Hearing the whimpering and cries of "no", the situation was becoming unbearable to those listening outside.

Suddenly, the figure of the man started to go down on the figure that was lying down. The Sergeant didn't wait for the man to get all the way down - he burst into the tent.

"William Thomas, I am arresting you for the attempted rape of Diane Giles, and I must warn you that anything you say may be taken down and used against you," he said, as he wrenched the man's arm up behind his back.

"Get your hands off me! You are interfering with God's will," William Thomas exclaimed with some rage.

"Wrong," the Sergeant said. "I'm carrying out God's will."

Julie and Angie got down beside Diane and helped her to sit up. She put her arms around Julie and put her sobbing head on her shoulder.

"There, there," Julie said. "Come with us; you don't have to stay here. Have you got some more clothes you can put on?"

"She isn't going anywhere," one of the women said. "She is staying here with me."

"I'm afraid you won't be here," the Sergeant said, "as I am arresting you for aiding and abetting an attempted rape, and that goes for you as well," he said to the other woman.

The Sergeant instructed PC Adams to deal with the two women, as Julie and Angie went with the girl to a small caravan, so that she could get dressed.

"Make sure you keep your clothes on this time," Julie said to the PC as they went out of the tent.

The Sergeant took Viceroy, or William Thomas, over to his bus to get dressed. As he put his clothes on, he turned to the Sergeant. "You are making a big mistake; if you go ahead with this, I will show everyone these photos." He placed them down in front of the Sergeant.

"If you think something like that would stop me from throwing the book at you, you're totally mistaken. If one of my officers was stupid enough to let someone take his clothes off, then that's his problem. He has to face the circumstances. Now get your clothes on and come with me."

They all walked down to the farm to where the police car was parked. When they got down to the farm, Julie said Diane was going to stay with her. The Sergeant took a piece of paper out of his pocket.

"This is her father's phone number," he said. "I think you should phone him, but don't go into much detail."

"I will," Julie replied with a little smile.

The Sergeant put the three main suspects into the back of the car. PC Adams started to get in the front. "Where do you think you're going?" the Sergeant asked. "Get on your bike!"

The Sergeant sped off in the police car. Julie and Angie took Diane in to meet Sarah. Then Sarah made them all a hot drink. "Can I use your phone a minute?" Julie asked.

"Of course; you know where it is."

Julie phoned Diane's dad. She didn't say what had happened, nor did she tell Diane that she had phoned him. He asked if he should come down. Julie agreed that he should.

John suggested that Angie should get Andrew to join them. Then John said he would go in to Tavistock to get fish and chips for them all.

"Good idea. I'll go with you," Fred said.

They soon got on their way, and it wasn't long before they were all sitting around the kitchen table eating chips and chatting about the goings on at the camp.

"What happens now to Viceroy?" Julie asked.

"I'm not sure," John replied.

"What do you think, Andrew? You must have some idea how these things work," Sarah said, just before putting a large piece of fish in her mouth.

"I'm not really sure, but I would think, as he was charged at the scene, he will probably be in front of the magistrate tomorrow, and they will decide if he is allowed out on bail or not."

"I wouldn't think he would get bail," Julie said. "They should throw away the key."

"Or cut his balls off, as Cart would say," Sarah said with a laugh. She then looked at Andrew and quickly said, "Sorry."

"Don't mind me. If I tell the truth, I agree with him," Andrew said with a smile.

"What will happen to my mum?" Diane asked.

"I'm not sure. What she has done is very serious. I would think she will probably go to jail," Andrew said, trying to be realistic.

"I hope not," Diane replied.

"No one should do what she's done; it's even more sickening to think she could do it to her own daughter," Sarah said.

"I don't think she really knew what she was doing; I know she loves me and wouldn't do anything to hurt me."

"I don't think she thought she was doing any wrong," Andrew said, trying to reassure Diane. "I believe she thought she was doing God's will. I think Viceroy totally brainwashed her, and I think you are probably right; your mum does love you."

"I think if you give it a bit of time, your mum will realise her mistake, and she will be looking to you for forgiveness," Julie said, as she put her arm around the girl to comfort her.

After a number of cups of coffee and a lot more chat, it was getting late and they soon all returned home and to bed.

The next morning, Julie phoned Sergeant Gibbs to ask what was going on. He told her that Viceroy would be appearing in front of the magistrates at three p.m. He also said that he hadn't made up his mind about the two women. He was going to hold them for another day and get some professional advice. Julie asked him if they could go to the magistrate's court. He said they could.

Julie had just put the phone down when Sarah phoned to say that Diane's dad had arrived at the farm, and she had sent him down to the lodge.

"I better go get her out of bed," Julie said. She quickly put the phone down and ran up the stairs. "You have a visitor," she whispered to Diane, who was snuggled down under the bedclothes.

"Who?" Diane asked, looking rather puzzled.

"Just come down when you are ready, and you'll see," Julie said with a smile. She ran downstairs to meet Diane's dad.

"Hello, I'm Sam," he said as he got out of his car.

"Come on in; Diane doesn't know that you are coming. She is just getting out of bed," Julie said, leading him into the front room. "You must have left very early. Would you like a coffee or something to eat?"

"A cup of coffee would be fine," Sam said very softly.

The kettle had boiled, and Julie was making the coffee when Diane came into the kitchen. "Who wants to see me?" she asked, looking around the room.

"Take this coffee into the front room; then you'll see," Julie said with a smile.

Diane took the cup into the front room; suddenly, there was a crash, as she dropped the cup of coffee at the shock of seeing her father. "Dad!" she said, with a mixture of surprise and excitement.

She ran to him and put her arms around him. Tears were running down her cheeks.

Julie entered the room after hearing the crash. Diane turned and looked at her. "I'm so sorry," she said. "I'll clean it up."

"Don't you worry about that; you look after your dad. I'll clean it up," Julie said. Her face was just beaming at the sight of Diane with her father. "I have to go over to the lodge and help them finish the breakfast - egg and bacon for both of you is it?" she asked, as she finished wiping the floor.

"You're too kind," Sam replied with a smile.

"I'm pleased to see you," Diane said. "I have had an awful time." She started to cry.

"*Shh, shh*, come on. I'm here for you now; it's all over now. I would have come for you before, but I had no idea where you had gone."

"I did try to phone you a couple of times, but Mum stopped me." She took a letter out of her pocket. "I wrote this, but I had no money for a stamp." Sam took the letter and started to read it; his eyes soon filled up and tears ran down his cheeks.

"Well I'm here now, and will look after you like a good father should."

"You are a good father, which is more than I can say for my mother. She was going to - " Diane paused. "Well, you know," she said.

"Don't judge her too hard. Your mother always was easily led, quite vulnerable in fact. I don't believe she really thought she was doing any harm."

Diane started to cry. "What do you think will happen to her? Could she come back and live with you?"

"I don't know about that; she broke my heart too many times. There is only so much forgiveness a man has."

"Why, has she done something like this before?"

"Not quite so drastic, but there have always been men."

"I'm sorry. I didn't know."

"We always hid it from you. God, I loved her. But do you know how it felt going out in the village and hearing people talking - saying what your wife had been up to and men sneering - I knew what they were thinking: 'I had his Mrs last night'."

With that, George entered the room. Julie said, "Breakfast is ready."

"And I'm to show you where," George said, beaming all over his face.

Back at the Tavistock police station, Sergeant Gibbs had Spud up in the interview room. A constable brought Spud in and sat him down.

"Hope you had a good night sleep," the Sergeant began. "What do you know about Bill Thomas? Has he been holding any of those women against their will, or forced them to have sex?"

"Look, there were things he did that I didn't agree with, like that girl they kept locked up for months, but what he did and what I have done are two different things. I just tagged along for the journey."

"Some journey, helping yourself to things that didn't belong to you, then saying it was God's will. You never believed that," the Sergeant said, as he put away his notebook.

"What else was I supposed to do? I had to live," Spud said, as if he had done no wrong.

"Have you ever thought of work, or don't you think you should do that?"

"Never did get on well with that; never had a job that suited me. Always seemed to be someone telling me what to do," Spud said as he scratched his head.

"That's what is supposed to happen; now what am I going to do with you? I should throw the book at you, but something tells me I should try and help you, not for your sake, but for those kids of yours."

"I don't know what would happen to them if I went to prison. They would just end up on the streets." Spud was trying to get the sympathy vote.

"Where do you think you all are now? You aren't exactly living the high life."

"I do know that, but what am I supposed to do? I have no house, no money."

"Look, against my better judgment, I will let you go, on the condition that you clear up the field and get the others up there to move on out of the area."

"You have my word," Spud said, as he held out his hand to the Sergeant.

"I hope you are a man of your word," the Sergeant said. He shook his hand.

Now for the women, he thought.

One of the constables went down to the cells and

brought both women up to the interview room and had them sit down on two chairs placed on one side of a table. The Sergeant came back in and sat down at the table opposite them. "Tell me," he said, "do you know what the sentence is for attempted rape, or even aiding and abetting?"

"No," one of the women said very quietly.

"I'll tell you, shall I? Five to twenty years in jail, that's what."

The woman who was Diane's mother started to cry. "I'm so sorry," she said.

"Sorry - how the hell could you do something like that to your own daughter?"

"I don't know. I feel awful; Diane will never forgive me. I think it would be better if I was locked up."

"On one hand, I feel you should be too, but my other hand says it would not be of any benefit. The thing is, if Julie and her friends at the farm hadn't worked out what was happening, and if we hadn't got there to stop it, you would be locked up, and I would have hoped they would have thrown away the key."

"I know. Why did we listen to that man?" Sally said, quite emotionally.

"We were fools looking for adventure," the other woman said, as she caught hold of Sally's hand on the table.

"Can I be sure that the pair of you are remorseful and won't do anything like this again? If that is the case, and you are prepared to give evidence against Bill Thomas, the police will not press charges, but your daughter might want to."

"I couldn't blame her if she did. She will never ever talk

to me again, will she? Oh, and yes, I will give evidence," Sally said, wiping tears from her eyes.

"I will too," the other woman said.

"Well, I will have to keep you locked up until after I have spoken to your daughter, which won't be until after Bill Thomas has appeared before the magistrate this afternoon." The Sergeant got up and beckoned to the constable to take them back to their cell.

Back at the lodge, Angie, Diane and Sarah had come down from the farm to see Diane. They all sat down in the visitors' lounge at the lodge, with Diane and her dad. Diane explained to Julie how she didn't think she could ever get over it. Yet she couldn't bring herself to hate her mother.

"It will be hard, and it will always be in the back of your mind," Angie said. She told her some of the things that had happened to her.

"How do you ever live with that?" Diane's father asked.

"It's hard sometimes, but I have wonderful friends around me, and I have met a wonderful man who loves me for what I am," Angie replied, as she looked at Julie and Sarah and smiled. Just as she said it, Olive walked in the door. Angie walked over to her and put her arms around her. "And this," she said, "is my adopted mum, and I love her to bits."

"I loved my mum once; although I can't hate her, I don't think I could ever love her again," Diane said, as she caught hold of her dad's arm.

"What about you - could you ever forgive her?," Julie asked Diane's dad.

"It's easy to say no, but I have forgiven her so many

times. I must still have some feelings, although I don't know how I could ever forgive her for what she has done this time."

"What's going to happen to me now?" Diane asked.

"I will take you home with me; we will have to leave soon," her dad said.

"Do we have to? Can't we go somewhere else and stay for a while? I don't want to face anyone at home; there will be too many questions," Diane said.

"You are more than welcome to stay here," Julie said, "you, Diane or the both of you."

"Please Dad, can we stay? I have some great friends here, and that's what I need now," Diane asked with pleading eyes.

"Are you sure you don't mind?" Sam asked Julie. "I have taken a fortnight's holiday from work."

"That's settled then. I'll get beds made up for you both. Would you mind sharing a room with Jenny?" Julie asked Diana.

"Not at all - she's the girl who is always with George, who we met at Sarah's, isn't she?"

"That's her; that's our Jenny," Julie said with a smile.

Things were all cleared up. Angie asked who was going in to the court. "Just me and Julie," Sarah replied.

"Is it all right if I come with you?" Angie asked.

"Of course," Sarah replied. "John will drop us off about one thirty."

"Is it all right if I take Dad up where that big pool is?" Diane asked Sarah.

"Of course, that's Julie's meadow," she replied.

"If you have some thinking to do, that's the place to do it," Julie said with a smile.

Diane and her dad left and made their way up through the fields to Julie's meadow. Sarah helped Julie clear up down at the lodge. Both of them were rather nervous about going to court; it was as if they thought that they had done something wrong.

Chapter Nineteen

That afternoon, John dropped Angie, Julie and Sarah outside the court. The three of them entered the court very nervously.

They sat in a row of seats that were there for the members of the public, and they were the only people there. Everything was very close. They would only be a few feet away from the magistrate. The three of them thought about leaving, but before they had a chance, a door at the side opened and in came Bill Thomas, handcuffed to a police constable. He was led into an area in the court that was surrounded by wood; it looked like it was just big enough to stand in. Then three men entered the court. One of them was Sergeant Gibbs. He and another man stood on the right-hand side of where the three were sitting; the other man went to the left of them. Everyone was standing when the magistrates walked in from a door that was up on a platform in front of them, and they sat at what looked like a large polished wood desk.

"Please sit," the one in the middle said.

"That's Lord Salmon," Sarah whispered to the others.

Just down in front of where the three of them were

sitting, there was another man, and it soon became clear that he was writing down everything that was said.

The magistrate in the middle asked, "Would the defendant please give his name, address and date of birth?"

"Viceroy - my date of birth is the 21 November 1961, and my address is wherever God takes me."

"Does anyone represent this man?" the magistrate asked.

"I do," the man sitting on their left said.

The magistrate looked at him over the top of a pair of gold, horn-rimmed glasses. "I suggest you tell your client that he is not helping his cause if he doesn't answer correctly. Now will you tell him that we need his correct name, address and date of birth?"

The man looked at Bill Thomas. "Will you please tell his lordship the name you were born with and your correct date of birth?"

"I was born twice. The last time I was born was in 1961, and the name God gave me was Viceroy."

"Perhaps it would be better if you gave us your date of birth the first time you were born and your name then," the man said calmly.

"William Thomas, 12 March 1936," he replied quite regimentally.

"And your address?" the man asked.

"No fixed abode," he replied.

"Now perhaps we can get on," the magistrate said. He turned to the Sergeant and asked him to read out the charges.

"Yes my lord," he replied. "It is alleged that on the night of 12 October 1964 William Thomas did attempt to rape a sixteen-year-old girl."

"Thank you. Is there any plea at this time?" the magistrate asked.

The man to the left said, "My client will be pleading not guilty to the charge, and we will be asking your lordship to grant bail."

"Is there any objection to bail?" the magistrate asked.

The man to the right, who was yet to speak, got to his feet. "My lord, I represent the prosecution in this case, and we strongly oppose bail due to the seriousness of the case and also due to the fact that the accused has no permanent address."

The magistrate turned to the man on the left. "What do you say to that?" he asked.

"My client is quite prepared to stay in the area, and he is certain that he will be able to prove his innocence. People might think it morally wrong, but he was just having a bit of adult fun."

The man on the left got up and interrupted. "My Lord," he said, "a girl screaming 'no, no, no' and crying is not adults having fun."

The magistrate said, "Can I remind the pair of you that this is not a trial, and your comments would best be saved for that trial. We are solely here to decide if there is a case to answer and whether bail should be granted." He then turned to Sergeant Gibbs. "It was you that arrested our council chairman, wasn't it? Does he not say he was just introducing people to adult games? Are you sure you are not letting your moral beliefs cloud your judgment?"

"I do not think stopping women from being treated like a piece of meat has anything to do with morals, my Lord," the Sergeant replied. "Women should be treated like human beings, as everyone should be, and if I did not take people like our council leader and this man here off the streets, I would be failing in my duties as a police officer."

The magistrate looked at the man in the dock. "William Thomas, I find it difficult to find a reason not to give you bail," he said.

Before he could finish what he was saying, Angie jumped up. "I'll give you a reason!" she shouted.

"Sit down," the Magistrate said firmly.

"No, not until you have heard what I have to say!" Angie again shouted.

"I will not tell you again. Sit down or you will be removed."

"I don't think that very wise, do you Doctor Fidgety Fingers?" Angie asked, this time quite softly.

The magistrate choked quite loudly and stared at Angie. "Come here. What did you want to say?"

Angie went over and stood on a chair, which took her up to the same level as the magistrate. She whispered in his ear, "If you give this man bail, I will tell the whole of the town what you've been up to, Doctor Fidgety Fingers; I could start right here."

"No need for that - now, please sit down," the Magistrate said.

The magistrate took a large gulp of water. "Now where was I," he said. "Oh that's right - William Thomas, I believe I would be failing in my duty if I did not put you on remand; you will be kept at her majesty's pleasure for a month. Then you will appear before us again, when a trial date will be fixed."

The magistrate stood up and left the court through the door to the rear of them. Julie nudged Angie as she sat down.

"What was all that about?" she asked with a smile.

"Let's go and get a coffee," Sarah said. "You can tell us all about it."

"We can have coffee, but I'm not telling you anything," Angie said quite sternly.

"We'll see about that," Julie said. She linked her arm to Angie's as they left the court and made their way to the cafe.

"Come on, spill the beans," Sarah said, as she linked her arm to Angie's on the other side.

"I don't think you better listen unless you can cover your baby's ears," Julie said with a smile, as she opened the door to the cafe and sat down.

Sarah ordered the coffees and then put her hands on each side of her tummy. "There," she said, "baby's ears are covered, and we are sitting comfy, so now tell."

"I don't want to; I want to forget all about it," Angie said firmly.

"I think you are a spoilsport. We just want to know about Doctor Fidgety Fingers."

"I don't want any of this to get back to Andrew. He never mentions anything about what I did, and it must be hard for him, but I would hate it if he knew that people he knew had visited the house. It is bad enough for him that his brother-in-law ran the operation."

"Our lips are sealed. Now, what about Doctor Fidgety

Fingers?" Julie asked, as she lifted Sarah's hand and put it back on her tummy.

"Well, your lord what's-his-name, known to me as Doctor Fidgety Fingers, used to wear a doctor's long white coat. He always had all the buttons undone down the front, with nothing on underneath."

"That must have been a frightening sight," Julie said. She pulled her chair in closer to the table.

"What about the fidgety fingers?" Sarah asked.

"He would come over and ask where the pain was; we were always told we had to play along with him. But I would trick him. I would say it was in my toe, and it was spreading. He would say, 'Anywhere else?' So I used to say, 'You start there, and I will tell you'."

"Was he content with that?" Julie asked, in a puzzled way.

"No," Angie continued, "I would then say, 'I think it's moving up my leg; my shins are hurting now.' He would then rub my shins; I would go on like that until he was just above my knee, then tell him he had rubbed too hard, and the pain had gone all the way up to the top of my arm."

"That bypassed where he wanted to land," Sarah said with a bit of a giggle.

"If I could keep it up for about five minutes and let him get close to my breasts, then close to my thighs again, he would get so excited that it would all be over before he even got what he really wanted."

"Bloody hell - have you any more stories like that?" Julie asked.

"Plenty, but I'm telling you no more, so drink your

coffee," Angie said. Just then, a car horn blew outside; it was John, who had come to pick them up.

"You are saved by the horn," Sarah said, as they all drank their coffee and went out to the car.

Back at the farm, Sergeant Gibbs was talking to Diane and her dad. "I haven't yet charged your mother or let her go; I want your reaction on the situation first," he said.

Diane started to sob. "I don't want to see her, nor do I want her locked up. I have never been as terrified as I was that day. How could she have done that to me?"

"I don't know what to say," Diane's father replied. "I have forgiven that woman so many times, but this - how can I ever forgive her? It would be dreadful if it was someone else's child, but to do this to your own - it sickens me."

"I quite understand. Her only saving grace, as far as I'm concerned, is the fact that she has accepted that what she has done is totally unforgivable - and she will be a witness against William Thomas," the Sergeant said.

"Do you think she was hypnotised or something?" Diane's dad asked.

"I don't know about that, but he certainly had them all under some sort of spell," the Sergeant replied.

"I think there was something. I don't believe she would have done what she did to me if she really knew what she was doing. By the way, what has happened to Spud? He is a bit of a rogue, but he and his wife tried to help me. None of the others would listen. I hope he's not locked up," Diane said as she dried her eyes.

"No, he has promised me that he will clear the site and

move them all on, and I believe him," the Sergeant replied.

"Look, can I have a word with Sally?" Sam asked. "I just want to see if I can understand what possessed her to behave like that."

"Of course you can if you think it will help the pair of you get over it. Am I to understand that you don't want me to press charges against her?"

"I can't see how we would get any benefit by seeing her in jail," Sam replied.

Diane just nodded in approval.

"I'll tell you what I'll do. I'll keep her in the station until after you have been to see her, and then I'll give her a while for things to sink into her head before I let her go. I have until seven o'clock tonight before I have to do something." The Sergeant tipped his helmet and left.

It wasn't long before Julie walked down to the lodge after arriving back from the court. Sam told her that the Sergeant had been out to see them and that he was going in to see his wife.

"Good luck," Julie said with a smile.

"Is Diane all right here with you?" he asked Julie.

"Of course - Sarah and I are going over to Angie's, so Diane can come with us." Julie spoke with a little excitement in her voice. "When we dropped Angie off, Andrew - he's the local vicar - was there to meet her and was very excited about something. So we thought we would give them a few minutes, and then go see what it's all about."

Sam left and went on into the police station. Julie and Diane made their way up to meet Sarah and walked over to

Angie's. "Come on, what's all the excitement about?" Julie asked as the three of them walked into Angie's cottage.

Andrew and Angie were sitting on the sofa. "Can I tell them?" Angie asked. She looked at Andrew with pleading eyes.

"Of course you can," he replied, smiling like a Cheshire cat.

"Well come on then," Sarah said. She could see Angie was overflowing with excitement.

"The bishop came to see Andrew this morning, and he told him that we want to get married. The bishop said there was no reason why we shouldn't get married in the church, and he would marry us if we wanted him to."

"Congratulations!" Sarah shouted. She gave both Angie and Andrew a kiss.

Julie went straight to Andrew. "I'm so pleased for you," she said, as she put her arms around him and gave him a big hug.

"Have you made any arrangements?" Sarah asked.

"No, but I would like to think we could get something sorted out sooner than later," Andrew said. You could tell it had made his day.

Chapter Twenty

A week had gone by since Andrew and Angie had announced their intention to get married. Sally's mother had gone to live in a flat in a big house on the other side of Tavistock. Spud had nearly finished clearing the site where the travellers were.

Julie and Fred, Diane and her father, Andrew and Angie where all up at Sarah and John's sitting around the kitchen table discussing the wedding.

"First things first," Sarah said. "Have you set a date?"

"Yes, just spoke to the bishop before we came over. December the tenth looks good if we can get everything sorted by then," Andrew said. He was now looking rather nervous.

"I don't see that as a problem; after all, we are all here to help," Julie said with a large smile.

"And I know Cart and Olive would want to get involved," Sarah said, as she was passing around cups of coffee as usual.

"Talking about Cart, do you think he would give me away if I asked him? He's been like a father to me since I came here."

"Do we think?" Julie asked with a thrill in her voice. "He will be overjoyed!"

"And what about you, Diane? I know I haven't known you for long, but will you be a bridesmaid?"

"Can I Dad?" She looked right in his eyes. "Please, please Dad," she pleaded.

"I'm not sure if we will be able to come down or not," he replied.

"I don't ever want to leave here," Diane said sadly.

"We have to; we can't impose on these good folk, and besides I have to go back to work," Sam replied.

"What do you do for a job?" John asked.

"I drive a lorry for a local corn merchant," Sam replied.

"Would you consider moving if you had a job down here?" Fred asked, as he knew Diane didn't want to go back home.

"It's not that simple; we have a council house, and it would be difficult to get somewhere to live down here."

"That's easy," snorted Sarah. "We have an empty farm cottage for rent, and I also happen to know that our local corn mill has a driver retiring, and I'm sure I could put a good word in for you if you wish." Sarah and John had taken a shine to them both.

"Say yes Dad!" Diane got up and hugged John. "Thank you, thank you, thank you," she said.

"I would like to thank you too. You are all so kind, but I will have to think about it," Sam said. He held his hand out for John to shake.

"There now Diane, you will have to work on your dad tonight," Sarah said with a smile.

"Oh trust me, I will," she replied.

"Going back to the wedding, would we be able to have

the reception down at the lodge?" Andrew asked Fred.

"Of course, we wouldn't want you to have it anywhere else," Fred replied.

"And in the evening, I thought we could all go up to Julie's meadow and light a candle," Andrew said, as he looked at Julie and smiled.

"Who are you going to have as best man?" Sarah asked.

"That's where I'm going to break away from tradition," Andrew replied. "I'm not having one."

"Are you sure? I thought you had to have one," Julie said, looking surprised.

"I think I can do what I like, and I'm hoping if she will do it, I'm going to have a best lady," he replied with a grin.

"That's very nice; I'm sure your sister will be thrilled," Julie replied.

"Oh it's not my sister I want; it's my best friend. So will you do it Julie?"

"What, me? Oh Andrew, I would love to! Are you sure you want me to do it?"

"There are two things I am really sure of. The first, the person I love and want to marry is Angie. Secondly, the friend I love and want for my best man is you." He leaned across the table and kissed Julie on the cheek.

"I just don't know what to say. I'm so excited! Have you any more surprises?" Julie asked as she got up to give Angie a hug.

"No, I think everything else is quite straightforward. We want George to be an usher, and I think Jenny should be a matron of honour rather than a bridesmaid, and then there's you, Sarah. I want you for a matron of honour, but Andrew was afraid that you might not want to in your condition."

"Don't worry about my condition. I would be honoured to be a matron of honour. Are there any other bridesmaids?"

"Just Diane and Amy," Angie replied.

"I have a few bottles of Gilbert Lanes cider in the back room. I'll go get them, and we can raise a toast to the lovely couple," John said. He got up and left the room. He soon returned with some bottles in his hands and some under his arms.

The rest of the night was spent drinking cider and talking about the wedding. The farmhouse was overflowing with excitement; it was late before everyone left to go home.

The next morning, there were one or two sore heads around. John was struggling with his work around the farmyard when Spud pulled up in his van with caravan behind.

"I just thought I would get you to check the field," he said. "Everyone has gone, and I've cleared up all the mess."

"Thanks for that," John replied.

"I promised the Sergeant I would, and I am a man of my word."

"Where will you go now?" John asked.

"Not sure yet," Spud replied.

"Ever thought about getting a job?"

"I'm not sure work suits me," Spud said with a laugh. "I have tried it before, but it didn't seem to work out somehow."

"It just seems a shame. You have two lovely kids. I'm sure

they would be happier if you stopped in one place," John said. He was joined by Sarah.

"What's going on?" Sarah asked as she approached them.

"I'm just trying to explain to Spud that I think his children deserve a better life than what he is giving them."

"Does your wife like this life?" Sarah asked.

"No, she doesn't," came a voice from the farm gateway. Spud's wife had left the van and was walking over to them.

"Hello," Sarah said, as she walked over towards her.

"It's all my fault," she said. "I thought that bloody Bill Thomas was some sort of god; what a fool I've been."

"You weren't the only one by all accounts," John replied.

"That's little comfort," she said.

"Look, I could give you some work if you want to stay a bit longer," John said, as he turned to look at Spud.

"Why would you do that? I pinched flowers and things from the village, and I nearly stole some of your lambs."

"I think there's more than that to you. Besides, in a funny sort of way, there's something about you I quite like. Just out of curiosity, what would you have done with the lambs?"

"When I was in Tavistock, I noticed someone had an advert in the post office for orphan lambs, so I was going to give them a call. I didn't let them go because the police were there, you know. After I loaded them up, I just couldn't take them, so I let them out in the lane."

"See, I knew you weren't all bad. Now, what about a job?" John asked.

"I promised the Sergeant I would move on, so I think I will go and see if I can find somewhere in the woods to park up, and then I can try my real passion, firewood," Spud said with a bit of a chuckle.

"If it's wood you want, I can help you there; we've got fifty acres of the stuff, and the trees are a mess. I'd like to see the woods thinned out and the big mature oaks and chestnuts left tall, with plenty of room for people to walk around and enjoy them."

"You sound like a man out of my own heart," Spud replied. He turned to his wife. "What do you think - would you like to stay?"

"You know I would. I'm just tired - tired of being called names, tired of wondering if the police are coming, and tired of the children not getting an education."

"That's sorted then. You can park your caravan down at the old sawmill, and if it all works out, you can move into one of the farm cottages if you like," John said, as he shook Spud's hand.

"I don't know how to thank you," his wife said, with a tear in her eye.

Over at Angie's cottage, Angie was out early to go over to Cart and Olive's to fetch Amy for school. Angie also wanted to use the opportunity to ask Cart if he would give her away. It was also apparent that Andrew had spent the night at the cottage.

Angie skipped across the road to Cart. "Bugger me, you're full of good spirits this morning," Cart said as Angie got to the door.

"I sure am. I have something to ask you."

"What's that then?" Cart asked in a surprised voice.

"Let me come in, and I'll tell you," Angie said. Her voice was sort of teasing.

As they entered the kitchen, Olive said, "You're early dear. Amy hasn't finished her breakfast yet." She put a glass of milk in front of Amy.

"I wanted a word with you two," Angie replied nervously.

"Nothing wrong dear, is there?" Olive asked.

"Oh no - I need to tell you that Andrew and I are to be married on December the tenth."

"That's wonderful! I'm so pleased for you both," Olive said. She was fussing around with Amy's breakfast.

"There is something else." Angie looked at Cart with her bright brown eyes. "I would like you to give me away," she said.

"What, me?" Cart asked, sounding surprised.

"Yes, you're the closest thing I have ever had to a father, and if I could choose a father, it would be you."

"I don't know what to say - of course I will if you are sure." The giant of a man had tears in his eyes.

"I have never been more sure of anything in my life." Angie then turned to Olive and asked her: "Will you fuss over me, argue with me, tell me I look beautiful, and be there for me on my big day, just like mothers do?"

"Of course I will. Come here and give me a cuddle - that's what mothers do when they are pleased for their children," Olive said, as she put her arms around Angie and gave her a big hug.

"Can I tell anyone?" Cart asked.

"Who do you want to tell?" Olive asked, with a frown on her face.

"The whole world" - Cart replied - "the whole bloody world!"

"That's something that will have to stop - all this swearing. You have responsibilities now," Olive said, quite crossly.

"Please don't change. I love you as you are," Angie said with a smile.

"You know, you are the second woman to have had an effect on Andrew," Olive said.

"What, was there someone else?" Angie asked.

"Oh, not like that, but before Julie came to the village, he was one miserable so and so. His sermons would send even the most ardent follower to sleep, and he never joined in with anything in the village. But after a few meetings, Julie brought the real Andrew out," Olive said, as she gave Angie another hug.

"He has asked her to be his best man, or women."

"Are you going away on a honeymoon?" Olive asked.

"We haven't even thought about things like that yet; we only started to discuss it last night," Angie said with a smile.

"Look at the time! Amy will be late for school," Olive said, as she started to get flummoxed.

Cart bent down and picked Amy up. "What do you think about Mummy getting married Missy?" he asked, as he swung her around.

"Does that mean I will have a daddy?" she replied.

"Yes darling, you will have the best daddy in the entire world," Angie said. She took Amy from Cart's arms and gave her a kiss.

"That's good because I've got the best Mummy, the best Nanny and the best Granddad, and now I'm going to have the best daddy. I'm lucky, aren't I Mummy?" Amy flashed a smile that would have melted anyone's heart.

"Yes dear, we are both very lucky to have such lovely people around us," Angie said. She grabbed Amy's coat and got her ready for school.

"You pair better get on over to school," Cart said, as his eyes were filing with moisture.

Angie left and ran with Amy over to the school.

Back over at the farm, Spud had come up to see John. "Would you come and see the Sergeant with me? I think I should explain why I haven't moved on."

"I'm going to market, so if you wanted to come with me, we could go see him then, if you like," John replied.

"I would very much appreciate that," Spud said. He held his hand out for John to shake again.

John told Sarah he was off, and he and Spud soon made their way to the police station. This only took a few moments, and it wasn't long before they were up at the market.

"I don't know if you just want to wander around a bit," John said. "I have to go over and pay my corn bill, and I'll meet you over by the sale ring in about half an hour." He fumbled in his pocket to make sure he had his cheque book.

John left Spud and attended to his necessary business. When he returned, Spud was by the sale ring. "Much gone through yet?" John asked.

"Not much - I've just been talking to that gentleman over there; he has his cart horse up for sale. He told me he can't make a living anymore," Spud said. The pair of them leaned on the rails around the sale ring.

"That's Harold Pope; he has been farming about thirty acres up on the moor. I heard he was packing up; the farm belongs to the prison, and they tell me they are having the land back," John said, with a tone of regret in his voice.

"He told me he advertised the horse for weeks, with no takers; he said he's only four years old." Spud sounded a bit despondent.

"I can't believe how things are changing so fast; the countryside will never be the same as it was when we grew up. How come you are so interested in old cart horses, anyway?" John asked.

"That's from my grandfather. He had a dozen of them pulling carts of lime around to the local farms and pulling timber out of the local woods. When he died, my father - the bastard - sold them for meat. Rationing was on at the time, and people never asked questions about what they were eating. I think that's what changed me. I so much wanted to carry on with what my grandfather was doing. I could never find a job to settle in." Spud's voice was gradually quivering as he spoke.

"People say you can't dwell on the past, but I do," John said. "But I am a realist as well, and although I modernise my farm, I will always do things to try and save our past," John said, as the horse entered the ring.

The auctioneer rose to his feet. "This is a beautiful four-year-old working horse belonging to Mr Pope. Mr Pope says if anyone buys the horse as a working horse, he will give them all the tack he has for him. So there we are; let's get her away whole; give me fifteen guineas, come on ten for him, come on two - I have one over there at the back from butcher Giles - is there any more because make no mistake I will sell him."

The auctioneer raised his hammer and looked around as if willing a bid to come. John suddenly raised his hand to make a bid.

"Two is it?" the auctioneer asked.

"No, I'll pay what he's worth," John replied, as he held both hands up to show ten fingers.

The auctioneer winked his eye. "I have a bid of ten guineas; can I see any more - and if you are all done, I will sell him - the last time then, sold to John Brite for ten guineas!" The auctioneer brought his hammer down hard on the rostrum.

"What are you going to do with him?" Spud asked John.

"Nothing, you are; this is the start of your timber business," John said with a smile.

"I don't understand you - why would you do that? I could just bugger off tomorrow, and you might never see me again," Spud replied.

"Two things - one, you aren't going anywhere until my wood is tidy, and the other - I felt sorry for the horse, not you," John said with a smile.

Spud smiled back. He knew for the first time in his life, he had found a true friend.

They left the ring and made arrangements to get the horse brought over to the farm, and they spoke to Harold

Pope about picking up the tack the following day. He seemed over the moon that John had bought him.

Whilst John had gone to market, Angie, Julie and Sarah had gone for their usual walk up to Julie's meadow.

"I can't believe how ravishing you look today," Julie said to Angie.

"It's the excitement of the wedding," she replied.

"I think it's more than that; a twinkle in the eye like that usually means something else," Sarah said, in a teasing voice.

"Oh really?" Angie smiled.

"Yes, I can remember when I saw a twinkle like that in Julie's eye." Sarah was still teasing.

"I can remember that as well, and you never left me alone until I spilled the beans," Julie said with a laugh.

"Oh all right then, if you must know, Andrew spent the night at my place last night, and if you want to know the details, I made love for the first time in my life. I might have had sex many times, but last night was the first time I made LOVE. My body ached, my legs shook, and my heart just fluttered. I have never had such feelings." Angie's face lit up like a million moonbeams.

Julie and Sarah both gave her a big hug. "I'm so pleased for you," Julie said.

Chapter Twenty One

Over. the next month or so, Spud made a great impression on the local community. He and his wife had moved into one of the farm cottages, and his two children had fitted in well. Alice, Spud's wife never left his side. She worked with him every day, whether it was in the woods with the horse, or out delivering wood.

Diane and her father had moved into the cottage next to Jan Symons, and her father had struck up a friendship with Jan and Cart. Diane was involved in all the wedding preparations along with Julie, Olive and Sarah.

Lenard James had been found guilty for not declaring that he knew people affected by the trial of Rupert Trelivan when he served on the jury. He was sentenced to six months in jail. There was still no decision on what was going to happen to Rupert.

So now the day had arrived. The church was all decked out with flowers. Angie was going to leave from the farm by horse and trap, the horse being driven by Spud.

Jan's old horse, Jess, also pulled a trap with the bridesmaids on.

Everyone was full of excitement, but the proudest man on that day had to be Cart. The smile on his face would have lit up the church, without the need of the candles that twinkled all around the church amongst the flowers. Olive had fussed all morning to get Angie ready and was still fussing when she arrived at the church - just like a mother would do.

The caterers had worked all morning at the lodge and had produced a banquet far beyond anyone's expirations. This was by far the biggest wedding that had been seen in the village, mainly due to Andrew's connection with the church in Tremarrow and the surrounding area.

Many a tear was shed throughout the service. With the service over, it was now time for the reception.

"Have you got your speech ready yet?" Sarah asked Julie, as they entered the lodge together.

"No, I haven't got a clue what I'm going to say," she replied.

"No doubt you will think of something."

"The problem is, I can't say much about Angie, so I will have to concentrate on Andrew," Julie said with a smile that looked full of mischief.

Sarah just smiled back.

Everyone had assembled in the lodge waiting for Andrew and Angie to arrive, and when they did, the applause echoed around the room. On the top table, Cart sat beside Angie, like a father would. Olive sat where a mother would. Andrew, having no living parents, had his sister sit where his mother would be. Angie had persuaded Andrew to do this, as his sister had hardly been seen since her husband had been arrested. Andrew had always said he knew he shouldn't talk so harshly, but it certainly brought the stuck-up cow down to earth.

With the meal eaten and the cake cut, it was now time for the speeches. The first to rise to his feet, standing in front of everyone like a proud giant, was Cart. He took a large drink from a glass that looked full of cider, and his words went like this:

"This will be short; I am the proudest man in the world today. To have the privilege of giving this beautiful lady away is something that I will remember for the rest of my life. I never found true love until late in life, even though it was on my doorstep the entire time. Had Olive and I gotten together earlier in life, who knows what might have happened. Perhaps we would have had a daughter of our own. There is one thing that is certain. I would have wanted her to be just like our Angie, and I know she could not have picked a better man to spend the rest of her life with. So I will ask you all to stand and raise your glasses to the bride and groom."

Everyone stood up, and the words *bride and groom* echoed around the room.

The next to rise to his feet was Andrew. "No sermons now!" one of the guests shouted out.

"I promise - no sermon," Andrew replied to the sound of laughter. He cleared his throat and began.

"If ever I doubted there was a God, any doubt I had was lifted from me the day this angel was sent to me. I think I fell head over heels in love the moment I saw her. I would like to thank Cart and Olive for acting like perfect parents.

I would also like to thank the beautiful bridesmaids. And not forgetting the beautiful matrons of honour, if you will all come forward and see Angie, she has a little gift for you. Whilst they are coming forward, I would like you all to stand and raise your glasses to the bridesmaids."

Every one stood up, and the word *bridesmaids* echoed around the room.

It was now time for the best man, or woman, in this case, to take the floor, and Julie rose to her feet. "Don't look so worried," she whispered to Andrew, as she cleared her throat and began.

"It's been nearly two years since I first met Andrew. I was told he was a grumpy man who kept to himself. But I found this was far from the truth. I believe I am a true Christian, although I don't attend church perhaps as much as I should. My views on religion are often quite different than Andrew's, but he has never told me that my perspective was wrong, and his was right, although we would sometimes discuss it for some time and just agree to differ. Anyhow, on to Andrew the man. I am proud to call him a friend, a man who has a great love of people, a compassionate man, a man who always puts others before himself, a man that will make a wonderful husband - oh, and father." (This brought a little laughter.) "He is a man who I am sure God is proud of, a man that everyone in this room has gone to for advice at some time or other. I'm not sure it was always good advice though…" (Once again, a little laughter rang out.) "So I will ask you all to stand and raise your glasses to my dear friend and his beautiful bride Angie."

Julie lifted her glass high in the air. "To the bride and groom!" she shouted, and the words echoed around the room.

With the speeches finished, and a few glasses of wine and cider drunk, darkness had fallen. Andrew got to his feet. "I would like once more to thank you all for coming, but we haven't quite finished yet. I don't know how many of you want to join us, but my wife and I, with our extended family, are going to Julie's meadow, where we will all light a candle in memory of our departed ones and our present loved ones."

Andrew and Angie left, with Angie still in her wedding dress and a large coat on. They wandered up through the fields to Julie's meadow, with all the guests following behind them. As all the guests left the lodge, George was at the door given everyone a candle.

When they arrived at the field gate and started to walk across the field, the sound of 'all things bright and beautiful' rang out. What neither Andrew nor Angie knew was that Julie had arranged for the Tavistock choir to sing. She had also arranged for Thistle and the Corn Flowers to play and sing.

Everyone was having a wonderful time and didn't notice Fred disappear with Sarah and Julie, but they certainly noticed them return with four large baskets of pasties.

This certainly was a wedding that would be remembered forever. It was the early hours of the morning before everyone had lit their candles and drifted home.

Chapter Twenty Two

With the wedding over, the village was now turning its attention to Christmas; Sarah was getting quite large, as it was only just over a month until her baby was due. Angie was doing a lot to help Andrew around the church. It had been decided to hold a carol service down at the lodge again this year and a Christmas day dinner for anyone who wanted to come. Angie said she would help this year, as they were all afraid of Sarah overdoing it.

It was now the night of the carol service. Cart had lit a fire, the same as last year. Andrew had asked Julie if she wanted to say a few words like last year. Spud had overheard this conversation and asked if he could say a few words. There were things he wanted to say, and this would be a great opportunity.

"I don't mind," Andrew replied, "but just remember it is a religious ceremony."

"Oh don't worry about me vicar, I won't let you down," Spud said.

Three local choirs had assembled down at the lodge. There was plenty of mulled wine and mulled cider, with an abundance of mince pies and pasties.

Angie, Julie and Sarah were all busy filling up glasses and

handing out the pasties and minced pies when they were approached by Gilbert Lane.

"What day are you coming over to see about your turkeys and tiddies?" he asked.

"We won't be coming to you this year," Julie replied.

"Why not - I've got the best around?" Gilbert said, with a touch of surprise.

"Because you tried to do us last year," Sarah said angrily.

"I just made a mistake; anyway, I gave you a fiver back to put things right," Gilbert said, as he pushed his cap to one side of his head.

"I tell you what - we will come and buy from you, but we will fix the price - how about that?" Julie said, with a smile that no one could resist.

"Yeah, but you might diddle me," Gilbert replied.

The three of them got right up close to Gilbert. "Now, would we do that?" Sarah whispered in his ear.

"I - I - I suppose I can trust you," Gilbert stuttered.

"Good, we will be over Tuesday," Julie said, still with that gorgeous smile on her face.

"That will be the tiddies sorted," Sarah said, as the three of them started to laugh.

There was suddenly a break in the carols.

"While the choirs are taking a short break, our most recent inhabitant would like to say a few words. I am sure you all know him by now, and know him as Spud," Andrew said, as he held his arm out for Spud to come over.

Spud jumped up on the seat that was facing the villagers. He cleared his throat, and then with full bounce and confidence, he began.

"You all know me by now, whether it's because I knocked on your door with some logs, or whether I nicked something from you when I first came here."

There was a sudden interruption, as there was a shout from the crowd: "You pinched my tiddies!" It was Gilbert.

Standing behind him, Cart put his hand hard on Gilbert's shoulder. "Carry on," he said to Spud with a little nod.

"Yes, I nicked your potatoes, and I'm sorry I also nicked flowers from the church and from local allotments, and I am totally ashamed of myself. I wasn't at the time; I just thought it was my way of life. I knew no other way. But meeting a wonderful couple changed my life, and of course you all know more about this wonderful couple than I do. I would like John and Sarah to come over here, so I can thank them publicly for what they have done, not only for me, but others as well."

Sarah and John went over and stood by Spud. Jan Symons came over and shook their hands. "I'm truly grateful," he said. Then Sam and Diane came over and shook their hands. Then a horse appeared, with Father Christmas on it. The horse was called Prince. It was the one that John had bought for Spud to use, and Father Christmas was Harold Pope, the man whose horse it was. Harold slid down off the horse. "Prince and I would like to thank you," he said, as he too shook John's hand and kissed Sarah on the cheek. He then returned to the horse and lifted a large sack off its back and brought it over. He put it down between John and Sarah.

"Open it," Spud said, with a large smile.

Sarah bent forward and opened the sack, and with the help of John pulled out a very large teddy bear. "It's beautiful!" Sarah exclaimed.

"Well, we wanted to get you something, but didn't know what to get, so we decided on something for the baby," Spud said.

"I don't know what to say; what a wonderful thought. I'm sure our little boy will be over the moon," John said, as he ran his hand over Sarah's tummy.

Spud then went on to say a big thank you to the rest of the village. "The people I was travelling with called themselves free lovers, but to be perfectly honest, they did not know the meaning of the word love. Love is what this village is all about - love for one another, not lust for someone's partner. Once again, a big thank you for accepting me and my family, and I hope we can spend the rest of our lives here."

"So do we!" Fred shouted, standing beside Julie, who had Spud's youngest daughter in her arms.

"I think you better stop now," Andrew said. "The choir want to start singing."

"Oh sorry," Spud said, as he came around to where Fred and Julie were sanding.

The choir started singing again, with everyone joining in; the evening was a wonderful success, and everyone went home happy.

The next thing of great importance was to get all the food organised for Christmas day, and of course the girls had arranged to go to Gilbert's on Tuesday. Angie had become a great friend to Julie and Sarah; it was now as if she had always been there, and on the Tuesday, the three of them started to make their way over to Gilbert Lane's. Sarah was driving the pickup. When they drove down past the church, PC Roberts was there; he held his hand up for them to stop.

Sarah wound the window down. "What's up?" she asked, as the PC came to the window.

"Doing a bit of traffic duty," he replied.

"What sort of duty?" Sarah asked, rather confused.

"I'm not really sure, but my Sergeant said it was time I used a bit of initiative. I asked what he meant, and he said I would end up on traffic duty if I couldn't find enough to do, so I decided I would show him what I can do. I'll get all our illegal drivers off the road, so can I see your licence please?" the PC asked Sarah.

"Why would you want to see my licence?" Sarah asked.

"So that I can see you are who you say you are, and check that you are legal."

"But you know who I am."

"I know that, but I can't be seen to be using favouritism, can I now?"

"Don't you think Sergeant Gibbs would think you a bit foolish for asking me for my license?"

"But how do I know you can drive if I don't see your licence?"

"How did I get here?"

"You drove here."

"Exactly, so I must be able to drive then."

"If you put it like that, I suppose you must have a licence."

"Look, I don't want to rush you, but we have an appointment," Sarah said. The other two girls had kept quiet the entire time they were stopped.

"Yes, I have finished with my check now. I'll stop the traffic while you pull out," the PC said, as if he had just achieved something.

The PC walked out into the middle of the road, held his hand up as if to stop the traffic, and then waved them out. The three of them gave him a little wave and then roared with laughter. "Did you see any traffic?" Julie asked sarcastically.

"Not seen a car all morning," Sarah replied, still laughing.

"Why didn't you just show him your licence?" Angie asked. She too was still laughing.

"Because I don't have one," Sarah replied.

"Bloody hell!" Angie replied.

"We have to make sure that as soon as the baby's born, she takes her test; she promised me she would last Christmas," Julie said with a tone of authority.

They had now arrived at Gilbert Lanes, who was quickly out to meet them. "Morning girls," he said.

"Morning," the three of them replied together.

"Do you want to see the turkeys first?" Gilbert said. "The trade price was three shillings and six pence a pound this morning."

"I thought we had a deal; we will decide the price," Sarah said firmly.

"I was just giving you an idea," Gilbert replied, looking like a man who wished he never had agreed to anything.

They went into a long shed, and on two long slate shelves were about a hundred turkeys, all plucked. "I think we should pick out six," Julie said.

"Yes, I think six twelve-to-fifteen pounders would be fine," Sarah replied, as she felt the turkeys' breasts.

"They are like you; three, good breasts," Gilbert said with a laugh.

"I think half a crown a pound is plenty enough to pay though," Sarah said. That soon took the smile off Gilbert's face.

"Don't be silly maid. Where can you get turkeys for half a crown a pound?" Gilbert asked, as he scratched the top of his head under his cap.

"Here," Julie replied.

"'Tis no good to take advantage of an old man; you said you would be fair."

"Will Ball has turkeys we could have for two and nine pence a pound, so perhaps we should go and see him," Sarah said, as she started to turn towards the door.

"Now, now, let's not get hasty; what if we said two and ten pence a pound? You girls be all right with that?"

"I think we could go along with that; don't you girls?" Sarah replied.

"What about tiddies then?" Julie asked with a bit of a giggle.

"I got good tiddies, three shillings a bag." Gilbert turned to Angie. "What a waste you made, you married to the Vicar."

"How do you mean?" Angie replied, with a look of concern.

"Well you know, vicars and that other stuff." Gilbert paused. "Vicars aren't exactly known for that sort of stuff."

"What stuff?" Angie asked angrily.

"Bed stuff," Gilbert said, as he wished it was something he hadn't started.

"I don't think that's a good enough explanation," Julie said, as she looked Gilbert straight in the eyes.

"Now, what about these tiddies?" Gilbert asked, as he tried to change the subject.

"I'll tell you about your tiddies. You can stick them the same place as you stick your turkeys because we are going over to get our stuff from Will Ball, and you can stay away from our farm and the lodge until you learn to respect people," Sarah said, as she shook with anger.

"Now I know you're only joking," Gilbert said. He started to laugh.

"Joking? How dare you think this is a joke? Come on girls," Sarah said, as they all turned and got in the pickup.

"God, I haven't seen you get like that since before Rupert got locked up," Julie said with a smile, as the pickup speeded out the lane.

"That bloody man ought to be locked up," Sarah said angrily.

"I think he's harmless, but thank you for getting me away from there. I did feel awkward," Angie said.

"He's not harmless. I wouldn't trust the fat ugly bugger further than I can see him," Sarah said, still shaking with anger.

The three of them went over to Will Balls and got everything they needed, except for the ham, which they had ordered from Mr Creabers in Tavistock.

Now with all the shopping done, it was time for the hard work to begin for the girls - Christmas dinner for more people than last year, fifty-six to be precise.

Of course there was more help this year, with Angie and Spud's wife Alice giving a hand.

Everything went off fine on Christmas day; it was now Boxing Day, and Fred had taken all the visitors down to the square, where everyone had gathered to see the hunt. "Do you like all this?" Spud asked Fred.

"Yes, suppose I'm a bit of a hypocrite though really," Fred replied.

"Why's that?" Spud asked with a surprised look.

"Well, I like all this, and make no mistake, if I see a fox at the chicken or lambs, I would have no problem with shooting it, but I can't see what enjoyment anyone can have in chasing a frightened animal for miles and miles."

"Funny that, that's the same thoughts that were going through my mind," Spud replied.

"Still, I suppose we can't have it all ways, and its things like this that make the countryside what it is," Fred said, as he got his group of visitors together.

Chapter Twenty Three

With Christmas over, and still no news of Rupert Trelivan, all the thoughts were now on Sarah's baby. "Would it be a boy or a girl? Would it be like John or Sarah? How heavy would it be?" Sarah had grown quite large and Olive said she wouldn't be surprised if it would weigh ten pounds.

It was a bright and sunny Monday morning in January; it was almost like a summer's day. They had no guests at the lodge, and Fred was going to spend the week decorating the whole place, so Julie was up early to see Sarah, who hadn't felt like going for a walk for a while.

But this morning, she was full of life. "Let's go up to the meadow," she said as soon as Julie arrived.

"Are you sure you're up to it?" Julie asked, a bit surprised.

"Never felt better. I just feel all shut in. I need to do something; all I'm doing is sitting around and getting larger and larger," Sarah said with a sigh.

"Well, it's a beautiful day, and I was going up later to fill the tin with candles," Julie said, as she opened her bag and showed Sarah how many she had.

"What, are you going to light the whole village up?" Sarah asked with a laugh.

"No. I don't know where they all go. I only filled the tin up a fortnight ago. I often wonder who goes up there besides us and Angie," Julie said as she closed her bag up.

"Ought we go over and call for Angie now?" Sarah asked as she put her coat on.

"No, she's doing the vicar's wife bit today, tea and biscuits with the bishop." Julie had a little giggle as she spoke.

"Come on then, let's go," Sarah said. She sounded quite excited.

They left and slowly wandered up across the fields towards Julie's meadow. "If you get that you want to turn back, say so," Julie said, showing concern for Sarah.

"Oh stop fussing. I'm all right; I have missed our daily walks like this."

They arrived at the meadow, walked over to the pool and sat down on the bank. "It's so peaceful," Julie said as she lay right back.

Sarah lay back beside her. "You will have to pull me up," she said with a large laugh.

"I love just looking up at the clouds moving by like little fluffy bits of cotton wool," Julie said like an excited child.

They had been lying there for about twenty minutes, when suddenly a voice came from close behind them. "My lucky day - two sluts here together - I couldn't have planned it better."

Sarah looked behind her. "Rupert, what the hell are you doing here?" she shouted.

"Come looking for you," he said, as he brandished a twelve bore shotgun from under his arm.

"What, have you escaped from prison?" Julie asked, as she got to her feet and bent down to help Sarah up.

"No, they let me out, so you see, I'm free to fight for what's mine - all the lies that you and people around you said about my mother." Rupert looked evil as he spoke.

"Why can't you accept that they weren't lies? I didn't ask for any of this, I didn't know Lord Trelivan was my father."

"No, your bloody mother encouraged him - took advantage of him, and now you are going to pay," Rupert said with an evil smirk.

"What is it you want - money? If so you can have it," Sarah said, trying to keep calm.

"Money - I don't want money. I want the same thing to happen to you that happened to my mother, and I have just the place for you."

Julie went straight towards him. "Can't you see she's pregnant, you big oaf? Why don't you just leave us?" she said with her voice raised.

Rupert hit Julie hard in the stomach with the butt of his gun. She fell to the floor quite winded. "Next time it will be your head," he said, quite softly as if he had done her a favour.

"You bastard," Sarah said angrily.

"Now, now Sarah, I call the names, not you," Rupert said, as he held the gun out and put the barrels under Sarah's chin.

"What do you want and how are you here?" Sarah asked, as she pushed the barrels of the gun to one side.

"I told you, I want you to suffer as my mother did. I have planned this ever since I have been locked up, but I couldn't have dreamed it would have been as easy as this."

"As easy as what?" Julie shouted, as she got to her feet, holding her stomach.

"As easy as finding you two here - now no more talking; just get up and walk through that gate. I haven't much time."

"Time for what?" Sarah asked.

"Never you mind, just get walking."

"We aren't going anywhere," Julie said, standing right up in front of Rupert.

"Really, then I will just kill you here," he said, as he stuck the gun up under Julie's chin and pulled the hammers back.

"No, just wait; we'll do what you want," Sarah said, with a pleading tone in her voice.

"Just take me. I'll do whatever you want, but please, please let Sarah stay here; you can see she can't move very well," Julie said, as she picked her bag up from the ground.

"Tough - now this is the last time I'm telling you, move." Rupert caught hold of Julie's hair and pulled her close to him; then he pushed her forward.

Julie stumbled. "Bastard!" she shouted.

"Now just keep walking." Rupert kept poking Julie in her back with the gun.

Sarah was finding it hard to walk; they had walked up through the next field and down around to the bottom of Stoney Moor quarry.

Sarah whispered to Julie in a frightened voice, "I think he's going to kill us here." She was now shaking with fear. Her thoughts were all about her baby.

Rupert heard what she had said.

"I won't kill you if you do what I say."

"Don't you realise you could be damaging Sarah's baby? You killed her last one. Aren't you satisfied," Julie said angrily.

"Always me - why do people say it's always me. If people minded their own business, no one would have had to die."

"That's easy to say; you killed your mother after treating her badly for years. Now why don't you just try and get your life together, and pray for forgiveness. Just let us go, and we won't tell anyone what has happened," Julie pleaded.

"Shut your mouth bitch. Now get over there." Rupert pushed Julie over by the old adit opening in the bottom of the quarry.

"This is all sealed off," Sarah said, as Rupert bent down and scraped a lot of grass back on the floor and produced a long metal bar from his pocket. One end was shaped like a key. He pushed down through a hole he uncovered in the floor in front of a thick metal plate.

"That's what everyone thinks, but I know different. I even had a mate of mine come down and see if it still works," Rupert said, as he turned the key. A small lever emerged from the ground. Rupert pulled it, and the large metal plate flew upwards and exposed a dark opening. "Now get in there," Rupert said in a rather calm voice.

"I'm not going in there," Julie said angrily.

"Oh really," Rupert said, as he caught hold of her hair and dragged her in. Sarah just followed. Rupert pushed Julie so hard that she went about ten feet into the mine. She fell hard to the ground. Rupert left, and the large metal door shut loudly behind him.

"What are we going to do?" Sarah asked, as she started to cry.

"Firstly, we don't cry. We get positive and find a way out," Julie said. She put her arm around Sarah to try and reassure her.

"I'm just worried about my baby. I don't want to lose it. That bloody Rupert, how did he get out?" Sarah was wiping her eyes; it was pitch black.

Julie placed her bag on the floor, took two candles out, pushed them in the soft ground and lit them. "We have plenty of candles," Julie said. She picked one of the lit ones up and started to glance around. "Gosh, it's massive in here," she said.

"Never mind that - how are we going to get out," Sarah asked with a tremble in her voice.

"I don't know, but there must be a way out somewhere," Julie said. She went back to the large metal door that had slammed down behind them and shone the candle all around it.

"Anything there to open it?" Sarah asked - more with hope than realism.

"No, Rupert would have made sure of that. This isn't our way out," Julie said.

"What are we going to do? If we can't open that door, we're doomed to die, along with my baby. Just like Rupert's mother - he's made sure we can't get out." Sarah started to cry.

"Right miss, you can quit thinking like that for a start. We have to think positive; the entire village will be looking for us. We have to keep calm. Let's walk in the mine a bit further and just set up a base," Julie said, trying to think positively.

Julie picked up her bag of candles and they walked further into the mine.

"Look," Sarah said, "a light on the floor."

They had come to a place that had a small speck of light on the floor; Julie stood on it and looked up about twenty feet above them. It was the start of a tall chimney that seemed to tower forever.

"Where do you think we are?" Julie asked.

"It's got to be the chimney down in the woods by the lodge," Sarah replied.

"This has to be our way out," Julie said, with a bit of excitement in her voice.

"How - we can't get up there," Sarah replied, with a tone that brought Julie down to earth.

"I know that, but look at all these bits of wood lying around. If we light a fire, someone is bound to see the smoke," Julie said, as she placed half a dozen candles around and lit them. She took her coat off and placed it on the floor against the side of the mine. "Come sit down here," she said to Sarah, who she could see was now in some discomfort.

"Thanks, but won't you be cold?"

"Not when you see the fire I'm going to have," Julie replied with a little chuckle.

"God, how can you keep so calm?" Sarah asked. "Aren't you afraid we might die?"

"I got too much faith for that. God will tell us when he wants us, and he hasn't called me yet," Julie replied, as she started to pick up loads of wood that were lying around. She placed them where the sunlight filtered down through the chimney. She bent down, and after a lot of blowing, finally got the fire to light.

The wood was so dry that the fire was soon roaring away; it was all that Julie could do to keep it from burning away.

Suddenly, Sarah shouted, "Julie, I'm all wet! I think my water's broken. What are we going to do?"

"I don't know, but we must not panic."

"Do you think they have seen the smoke?"

"No," Julie replied. "The wood is too dry, and there is no smoke."

"I've got pains now. I think my baby's coming."

"That's contractions; they can go on for hours. Your baby won't come yet."

"It is, I tell you - it is coming quick. Do something!" Sarah shouted.

"What - I don't know what to do."

"You helped my John with the lambs; it can't be much different," Sarah said in between loud groans and moans.

"Lie down, and I'll have a look and see if I can see anything" Julie said, still talking quite calmly.

"Well, what can you see?" Sarah was grunting and pushing.

"Bloody hell - there's a head," Julie replied. She gently put her hands up to it. "Now come on - one big push and you're there."

Sarah took a large gasp of breath, and with a gigantic push, the baby slipped out into Julie's hands.

"Is it there?" Sarah sighed.

There was a faint cry, as Julie said, "Yes, it's a beautiful boy." She handed the baby up and placed it in Sarah's arms.

Sarah smiled. "Oh, he's so beautiful." Sarah sobbed.

"Right, you hang on here. I'm going to look for a way out," Julie said as she stood up.

"I want to push again," Sarah said, this time quite calmly.

"Don't do that. You might push your insides out," Julie said in a worried tone.

"I can't help it; I think something is wrong. Please have a look," Sarah said as she started to groan again.

Julie got down on the floor in front of her again. Sarah started to groan loudly again.

"Bloody hell - there's another head!" Julie shouted.

Sarah pushed and pushed until the baby slipped into Julie's hands. There was no movement in the baby at all.

"What is it?" Sarah asked, sensing something was wrong.

"I don't know," Julie whispered, as she stood up and started to blow hard into the baby's mouth. Then suddenly, there was a bit of a gurgle. Julie held the baby upside-down by its legs and gently patted its back. Then suddenly, there was an almost deafening cry. Julie quickly turned the baby right-side up and cuddled it.

"What is it?" Sarah asked. A smile had come to her face.

Julie held the baby away from her so that she could have a look. "It's a girl" she said. She leaned forward and placed the baby into Sarah's other arm.

Sarah's face suddenly changed from a smile to tears. She looked at Julie and said, "What will happen to us now? We're going to die, aren't we?"

"No we are not - I am going to build the biggest fire you have ever seen under that chimney. I'm going to collect every bit of wood down here and anything else that will burn, and the smoke will be seen for miles." Julie looked up the chimney. "It's dark out now, so I will build the fire all night."

"My babies are cold, and I think they are hungry," Sarah said with a whimper.

"Well, you've got their food," Julie said. She took off her dress and ripped it in half, taking one baby from Sarah and wrapping her in half of the dress. Then she handed it back, took the other and wrapped the boy.

Sarah took the babies and let them feed, one on each side. The smile came back to Sarah's face. "Am I doing this right?" she asked.

"I wouldn't think there is a right or wrong way," Julie replied, as she lit a little fire in front of Sarah. "We will keep this one going to keep warm, and I'll start to build the big one."

Sarah looked at Julie in the dim candlelight. She had just noticed the skimpy panties and bra she had on under the dress she had removed. "I can see why Fred always has a smile on his face," she said.

"I think he will be disappointed tonight," Julie said with a little giggle. She was glad Sarah had found something to smile about.

"Where did you get them from? I have never seen anything like that - did you know you can see your entire bum cheeks?" Sarah asked.

"Yes, it's called a thong, and I sent away for it."

"Where did you send to? I haven't seen them in my Kay's catalogue?"

Julie laughed. "That's enough about my bum; you just

carry on and feed your babies," she said, as she started to collect stuff for the fire.

Chapter Twenty Four

***

Back at the farm, around lunch time, John was becoming quite concerned that Sarah and Julie hadn't returned. He walked down to see Fred. "Is Sarah here?" he asked.

"Haven't seen them yet," Fred replied.

"They seem to have been gone a long time, and I'm a bit concerned, especially with Sarah in her condition," John said with a worried look.

"You know what that pair's like. They could still be sitting there talking, not thinking about the time," Fred said in a reassuring voice.

"You're probably right, but I think I'll stroll up to the meadow to meet them," John said.

"I'll come with you," Fred said. He put the brush down that he was sweeping the yard with.

They both strolled up towards the meadow, expecting to find Julie and Sarah on their way down. But they arrived at the meadow, and the girls were nowhere to be seen. "You know what they've done," John said with a laugh. "I bet they went up to the top gate and walked down the road as we came up across the field."

"Yes, and I bet they knew we would walk up to meet them," Fred said with a smile.

The pair of them walked back to the farm chuckling away, but when they got back to the farm, their mood changed, as nether Sarah or Julie where anywhere to be found.

John and Fred were now getting really worried; they had been over to Olive and Cart's, and Andrew and Angie's, but no one had seen them.

Fred and John went back to the farm. "Do you think we should ring the police?" John asked Fred.

"I don't know. I'm not sure what we should do," Fred replied.

It wasn't long before quite a few of the villagers started to arrive at the farm, as news was going around that Sarah and Julie had not returned from there walk.

John phoned the police, and it wasn't long before Sergeant Gibbs arrived. "Are you sure you checked with everyone where they might have gone, because there's usually an explanation?"

"Quite sure," John replied in a worried tone.

"Well, the best thing we can do is to get everyone organised and do a sweep of the whole farm." The Sergeant arranged the villagers into groups.

Just as they were all ready to set off, Mr Knight drove into the yard. "What's going on?" he asked, as he got out of his car and noticed all the groups of people around.

John told him that Julie and Sarah had not returned from their walk and they were just about to start a search.

"I hope this isn't relevant, but I came over to tell you that they let Rupert out of jail this morning, pending a decision by the home secretary," Mr Knight said with a look of concern.

"That has to be the answer!" John said, shock registering in his eyes. "What do you think he has done with them?" He called the Sergeant over and told him what Mr Knight had said.

"There are conditions attached to his release; he has to live more than fifty miles away and has to report to a nominated police station at seven p.m. each night. He opted to live in London and report to the Bow Street police station."

The Sergeant looked at John. "Can I use you phone?" he asked.

"Of course," John replied, walking over to the door with the Sergeant following.

The Sergeant made a phone call and then announced that Rupert was put on the seven thirty train for London this morning.

"Did anyone else know he was coming out today?" John asked, still thinking Rupert was involved somehow.

"I don't know, but I will try and find out," the Sergeant replied. "But first we have to get this search under way, as we don't have a lot of daylight left."

The Sergeant organised all the villagers into groups of four and five and got some started by the lodge and some in the corner of the yard. Some went down to the river, and some went to the centre of the village. The plan was that they would all meet up at Julie's meadow.

After they had all gone on the search, the Sergeant went in to use the phone to see if he could find out any more information on Rupert's release. He had persuaded John and Fred to stay back at the farm; Angie and Olive stayed with them.

John put his head in his hands. "I suppose the Sergeant didn't want us to go on the search in case we found their bodies," he said, thinking the worst.

"It's no good thinking like that. I know Julie won't let Sarah come to any harm," Fred said, trying to put a brave face on the situation.

The search went on all afternoon, but to no avail; it had now become quite dark. Sergeant Gibbs had made inquiries into who had visited Rupert in jail; it turned out he only had one visitor on a regular basis, and that was Brian Furze. "I have my colleague Sergeant Smith going over to question him," Sergeant Gibbs said.

As the searchers all returned, Angie and Olive made them all cups of tea. "I can't help thinking we are missing something," Cart said, as he took a sip of tea.

"Just think dear; no one knows this place better than you," Olive said as she poured yet another cup of tea.

"Do you think if I walked the farm with you, something might click? I just think there is a simple explanation, and we are just missing them somewhere," Fred said.

"That's just what I mean," Cart replied. "I'll just get my big flashlight and we can do a sweep of their haunts."

It wasn't long before Cart returned. Fred went with him searching every nook and cranny. They went down to the bottom of Stoney Moor quarry and over to the old mine adit. "There are a lot of footprints around here; all the grass has been pushed down," Fred said, as he bent down with his face only inches away from the ground.

"I expect it is where people have been searching; that

large iron plate used to be a door," Cart replied, as he felt all around the outside of the iron plate.

"Do you think they could have got inside there?" Fred asked, hoping they had found the answer.

"No, it's impossible; this adit runs right through the hill to the other side. Old Grandfather Trelivan fitted the door after a fire in the mine. The fire was made worse by a through draft blowing right through the hill from the entrance on the other side. This entrance was blocked off with the large iron door; the door was put there rather than blocking it up, so if there was an accident, it could always be opened in an emergency."

"Is it worth us opening it?" Fred asked, as he too was feeling around the door.

"That's my point. We can't; you need the key, and there was only one ever made; my father made it, and it went missing from the wall of the big house when Lord Trelivan died last year. It was on show in the big hall."

"I still wish we could go in. I just have a feeling about this place," Fred said with a large frown.

"Come on," Cart said. "We better continue around the lodge and go back to the farm."

It was around seven thirty when they got back to the farm. Sergeant Gibbs had phoned the London police station again, and had been told that Rupert reported there at seven o'clock. Sergeant Smith arrived after he had interviewed Brian Furze, who said he was at Exeter market and was involved in a small accident at three o'clock. "I checked with the woman driver, and she confirmed that he ran into the back of her car when she left the market."

"I still can't help thinking that Rupert is behind it somehow," John said, as he held his head in his hands.

"It seems strange that they have gone missing the day Rupert was released from jail," Fred said, agreeing with John.

"I know this is difficult for you both, but there is nothing we can do until the morning. I will leave a couple of officers here overnight," Sergeant Gibbs said, as he put his hand on John's shoulder.

"I do understand. I can't see me going to bed, though," John replied.

"We will stay up together," Fred said.

"Me and Cart will stay as well," Olive said, as she put her arm around Fred.

"Angie and I are going nowhere either," Andrew said in a soft voice.

"I know we don't visit church very often, but Julie always says God will help when he can, but sometimes he's so busy he can't keep an eye on everyone," Fred said, putting his head in his hands. "Let's hope he isn't too busy tonight."

"I'm pretty sure God listens to Julie. I'm sure he is talking to her now, wherever they are, and he will give her the strength to survive whatever's happened to them," Andrew said in a reassuring way.

"I'm with you Andrew. I'm sure whatever has happened to them, Julie will get them out of it," Cart said.

Talk like this went on all night, with everyone sure that Julie would make sure they would survive, whatever ordeal they were going through. All night they would doze off in the chairs in the farm kitchen, and then they would all wake up and drink tea. It was the longest night of their lives.

Chapter Twenty Five

Back in the mine, Julie was working her butt off, dragging large bits of timber over under the chimney and stacking it up.

"Are you sure this is going to work?" Sarah kept asking, each time with more concern than the last.

Julie stopped for a moment and wiped her brow. She sat down beside Sarah. "Let me hold one," she said, taking one of the babies from Sarah.

"It's not myself I worry about; I just want my babies to survive," Sarah said as she started to cry again.

"Hey Mrs, that's enough of that. We are all going to survive; my fire will be so big that they will see the smoke for miles. Now here, have this little chap back, and I'll get on with my fire building," Julie said.

"I wish I could help you," Sarah said, wiping the tears from her eyes.

"You are doing fine. I think your babies know we are in trouble; that's why they aren't making a fuss. They haven't cried since they were born," Julie said. She made conversation with Sarah every time she brought more stuff back for the fire.

"Aren't they beautiful? I think the candlelight makes

them even more beautiful. John will be so proud of them."
Sarah was now beginning to think there was hope.

Julie still kept dragging larger and larger bits of wood over
to the fire. Where she got her strength from, only God
knows.

"Have you thought of any names yet?" Julie asked, as she
dragged what seemed to be a large oak beam.

"That's easy. My lovely little boy is called Fred, and my
darling little girl is called Angel, after you."

"That's lovely. Fred will be pleased, but I'm not sure where
the Angel bit comes from," Julie said with a little laugh.

"How much more are you going to pile on there?" Sarah
asked, as she looked up at the large mountain of wood.

"I'm going to take some candles and go a bit further in to
see if I can find something that will burn with a lot of smoke."

"Don't go too far; it might not be safe," Sarah said.

"I'll be all right; you just cuddle those little beauties in,"
Julie said. Sarah's mood had now changed to optimism.

Julie made her way deep into the mine. Water was
dripping all around her, her body was running with sweat,
and water was trickling on her from above. She suddenly
tumbled on some old rubber belting. It was so heavy that she
couldn't lift it. She managed to drag it a few feet at a time
until she managed to get back to Sarah.

"This will make some smoke," she said, as she collapsed
to the ground.

"Are you all right?" Sarah asked, as Julie was gasping for
breath.

"Yes, I'm fine. I just need to get this on top of the fire; it
will make the most smoke you have ever seen."

Sarah giggled a little as Julie struggled to get the rubber belting on top of the fire.

"What you laughing about?" Julie asked as she smiled back.

"Nothing, I was just thinking I bet there would be a queue of men ready to rescue us if they knew what you were wearing."

"I'd take the lot off if they would come now," Julie said with a laugh.

"I don't think you need to take anything else off - all the time I have known you, I never realised how beautiful you are."

"Hey, that's enough of that; you're getting me worried. You'll be saying you fancy me next."

"I would if I were a man; I'm sure of that," Sarah said with a laugh.

"What time is it?" Julie asked, as one of the babies started to whimper.

Sarah looked at her watch as she passed one of the babies to Julie. "It's midnight," she replied.

"I think little Fred here wants a feed," Julie said. She handed him back to Sarah and took Angel from her.

"I think you should come and sit down now, and try and get some sleep. What time are you going to light the fire?" Sarah asked.

"It's not light until around eight, and I'm sure there will be a lot of people searching for us. By the time everyone gets organised, I reckon about half past eight we should light it. I reckon it will take half an hour to get going and make smoke," Julie said as she cuddled Angel close into her chest.

"Well, we got eight hours to freedom little man," Sarah said, as she took out one of her breasts to feed him.

Once little Fred had a feed, it was Angel's turn. Little Fred slept in Julie's arms, and Angel in Sarah's. Neither of the little treasures could have any idea how their life began. Neither Julie nor Sarah slept much through the night, just a nod off here and there. Most of the night was spent with them talking about their past. Julie was back deep in the mine at around seven a.m., still bringing more fuel for the fire. The pile was now so large that Julie said Sarah and the babies should get much farther away.

It was now eight thirty, and Julie was ready to ignite the fire. She rested some long poles onto the small fire they had burning all night for warmth. As soon as they caught fire, she pulled them out and pushed them under the large stack of wood. Soon flames started to go up through the middle of the pile. It gradually got hotter and hotter until it became unbearable to be within thirty feet.

"I can't see much smoke," Sarah said, sounding rather concerned.

"It will in a minute once that rubber starts to burn; then you will see it roaring up the chimney," Julie said, her body glowing with the heat.

"Look," Sarah said, "the rubber, it's started to burn."

Suddenly, the whole place started to fill with smoke, and then suddenly it was like a whirlwind. All the smoke twirled around and then went up the chimney, as if being sucked by a huge force. "Hurrah!" they both shouted together.

Chapter Twenty Six

<hr>

Now the morning had arrived and daylight was just breaking through. Up at the farm, things were very tense. The villagers had started to assemble in the farmyard, ready to start another search. PC Roberts was out in the road when Sergeant Gibbs arrived. "What are you doing out here?" he asked.

"Directing traffic."

"What traffic?" the Sergeant asked, looking up and down the road.

"I just thought - "

The Sergeant interrupted. "That's the problem; you never think. Now get in the yard; you can help in the search."

They went into the yard where they were met by Fred, John and a group of villagers. "Can anyone think of anywhere we haven't searched yet?" the Sergeant asked.

"I know every inch of this place, and I believe we have covered it all," Fred said. "I still believe that bloody Rupert has something to do with it."

"I wouldn't be surprised if that Rupert had something to do with it," one of the villagers said.

"Let's not speculate. I can assure you Rupert is not involved," the Sergeant said.

Suddenly, Cart Shouted excitedly, "Look, look!"

Everyone looked to where he was pointing. Smoke was trickling out of the top of the old mine stack down by the lodge. The smoke grew more and more intense until it was belching out.

"What's under there?" Sergeant Gibbs asked.

"Stoney Moor Mine," Cart replied.

"I had a feeling about that place last night," Fred said.

"How do we get in there?" John asked with some urgency.

"There is only one key, which was stolen from the big house. If we take your pick-up, we can get my acetylene and cut a hole through," Cart said, as he put his arm around John. They headed for the truck.

"I think we should get the fire brigade and ambulance here, just in case," Sergeant Gibbs said as he picked up his radio transmitter.

"Come on," Angie said to Fred. "Let's get up there."

Andrew, Fred and Angie rushed up across the fields, with all the villagers close behind; there was also a number of media representatives there with them.

Sergeant Gibbs told PC Roberts to stand in the road to direct the fire brigade and the ambulance up to the mine entrance.

"I don't know what's right or wrong; it's wrong when I stand in the road, and now he tells me to…" the PC muttered as he walked out of the gate.

Everyone had assembled around the mine entrance. Cart

and John arrived with the cutting gear, and it wasn't long before Cart had the gas lit and was cutting through the door.

He first cut a small hole so that he was able to see if anyone was directly behind it. "Can you see anything?" Fred asked, as Cart turned the gas off and put the torch on the ground to take stock.

"No, but if I'm not mistaken, I can hear a baby crying," he replied.

"Bloody hell," John said in a shocked tone.

"Should I just cut a small hole to crawl through?" Cart asked.

"Just cut the whole thing out as quickly as you can," Fred said, as he picked up the cutting torch from the floor and handed it to Cart.

"We will have to make sure that if they hear us, they don't touch the door. Fred, you shine your torch through the hole and keep an eye out for them," Cart said. He then explained where he was going to cut, down each side, then along the bottom, and then across the top.

Inside the mine, Julie and Sarah were too far in to hear what was going on, but Julie suddenly got up and picked up one of the babies. "Come on," she said, "time to go."

"What do you mean, time to go?" Sarah asked.

"A voice from somewhere tells me there's someone outside waiting for us."

"Are you sure?" Sarah asked, surprised.

"I'm sure now; come on, just take it steady. Do you want me to carry the babies?"

"No, I can manage one and a candle," Sarah said, as she

stood up to take her first steps since the babies were born.

They moved slowly towards the entrance. "What are you going to do about clothes?" Sarah asked.

"I'm not going to worry about that now; let's just get out of here and get these little angels and you checked over," Julie replied.

They made their way out through the dark tunnel. "Did we walk as far as this? Are you sure we are going the right way?" Sarah asked, surprised at how far they were walking.

"I'm sure," Julie replied.

All of a sudden there was a tremendous crash. The large iron door had come crashing to the floor, just as Julie and Sarah were within a few yards of it. They both jumped, and the babies started to cry.

Fred and John stepped on the door immediately; it collapsed on the ground. The collapse of the door had caused a draft that blew out the candles that Julie and Sarah were carrying. They saw the opening. Sarah burst into tears.

John and Fred quickly led them outside to a round of applause. Cameras were clicking, and questions were being asked before Sarah or Julie could draw breath. Sarah looked at John in a real loving way. "It's time to meet your son and daughter," she said.

"They're beautiful," he replied. "Are they all right? Are you all right?" John was so concerned.

"Yes, we're all fine, but I never thought we would get out alive, and I don't think I would have gotten through it without Julie," Sarah said.

"Come now," John said. "You're safe now." He put his arm

around her, as Angie came over and took the baby from her.

Olive had taken the other baby from Julie, so Fred could give her a big hug.

When they broke away, Julie raised her arms towards the sky. "Thank you God," she said, as the cameras started clicking again.

Andrew came over and put his arms around her. "Thank God you're safe," he said. He then took off his coat and put it around her.

Sarah had nearly made it to the ambulance, with Olive carrying one baby and Angie the other. "I hope you don't mind, but I named our babies when they were born," Sarah said to John.

"Of course I don't mind, but I would like to know what they are," he replied with a big smile.

Sarah took the boy from Olive. "This one is Fred, after our special friend." She leaned forwarded and took the other one from Angie. "And this one is called Angel, after my Angel Julie, who saved our lives."

Sergeant Gibbs approached just before Sarah got into the ambulance. "Do you feel up to telling me what happened?" he asked.

"Rupert put us in there. How is he out of jail?" she asked.

"Don't see how he could - he was put on the train early in the morning to London, and he reported to a police station there," the Sergeant said, as he scratched his head under his helmet.

"Trust me, when you're looking into the eyes of someone holding a shotgun, you know who it is," Sarah said quite angrily.

Sarah, Julie and the babies left in the ambulance. John and Fred got the car and followed them.

Cart went over to the Sergeant. "I knew that bloody Rupert was behind this," he said.

"I don't see how though," the Sergeant replied.

"What if he wasn't on that train?" Cart asked, as he pushed his cap towards the back of his head.

"He had to be. I checked out all the train times. There was no way he could have gotten to London if he wasn't on that train," the Sergeant said. He had a real puzzled look on his face.

Mr Knight, the solicitor, was standing beside Cart and the Sergeant. "What if he didn't catch that train, and someone took him to Exeter to catch a later train? It's only three and a half hours from there by train, and there's one every hour," he said.

"That's it," Cart shouted. "Brian Furze - you said he was in Exeter, and I bet he stole the key to the mine."

"I think it's worth you investigating that," Mr Knight said.

"I think you're probably right," the Sergeant replied.

Chapter Twenty Seven

That night, Julie was home from hospital, but Sarah and the twins were kept in overnight.

The Sergeant didn't notify the London police station, as he didn't want to alarm Rupert. Besides, he wasn't going anywhere. He decided to question Brian Furze first, so he made his way over to his house.

"What do you want?" Furze asked, as he opened the door and saw the Sergeant.

"I want you to give me one good reason why I don't charge you with murder," the Sergeant replied, looking rather stern.

"Murder - what you talking about?" Furze replied.

"What I say - you better have some answers ready."

"Answer's to what? I don't know what you are talking about," Furze replied in a cocky way.

"Really - What about if I tell you that I know you stole the key that opens the mine door?" the Sergeant said confidently.

"Prove it. Anyway, what that's got to do with murder?"

"You don't know? It was used to open the mine door, where two people were locked in and left to die - no, in fact, four people."

"Four people - what four people?" Furze looked rather bewildered.

"Sarah Brite, her friend Julie and the two babies," the Sergeant replied with a face full of emotion.

"I know nothing about any babies," Furze replied.

"So you know something about something then." The Sergeant paused. "Let me tell you what I think happened, on the evidence I have. You stole the key from the big house for Rupert Trelivan, you collected him yesterday morning from Tavistock station, you then dropped him off up the lane behind Tremarrow farm, where you waited for him, and then drove to Exeter station, where he caught the train to London."

"You think you got it all sussed out, don't you?" Furze said, as he turned away from the Sergeant.

"You tell me that's not what happened."

"I'm telling you to prove it," Furze replied.

"No, I'm telling you, if I can't prove Rupert Trelevin was there, I'm going to charge you with attempted murder," the Sergeant said forcefully.

"*Attempted* murder you said - you mean they are not dead?" Furze replied, looking a little relieved.

"Lucky for you, they were rescued this morning, or it would have been murder. However, four charges of attempted murder will probably carry two life sentences," the Sergeant said, looking pleased with himself.

"You will never make it stick," Furze said, looking rather pleased with himself.

"We will see about that, Brian Furze. I am arresting you for the attempted murder of Sarah Brite and her two children. I must also warn you that other charges might follow. Anything you say will be taken down and used in court," the Sergeant said, as he took out a pair of handcuffs and slapped them on Furze.

The Sergeant took Furze back to the jail, and then he phoned the police station in London. They said that they would arrest Rupert the next morning at his address, and then an officer would bring him down on the train. He would arrive late in the afternoon.

The next morning, Sarah and the twins were allowed home. Angie, Olive and Julie were at the farm when she arrived. They had spent much of the night before making a large banner, which they had placed across the farm entrance. It read, "Welcome Home Clever Mum."

The farm kitchen was once again full of with joy and laughter. Cart came in, clutching a newspaper. "Who wants to see this?" he shouted excitedly.

"What is it?" Sarah asked, looking rather puzzled.

"This, this," he said, pointing to a picture in the paper.

"Well, we can't see from here," Julie said. "Bring it over here."

Cart came over and laid the paper on the table. There was a full page picture of Julie with her arms raised to the heavens when she had come out of the mine. Her skimpy knickers and low-cut bra left little to the imagination. The headline read: "Body of an Angel."

"I bet a lot of crib rooms will have that pinned up on the wall," Angie said with a smile.

"I'd be embarrassed if that was me," Olive said, as she picked the paper up and had a closer look.

"I don't mean to be rude dear, but your body would embarrass the photographer," Cart said with a chuckle.

"I'll remember that," Olive replied, as she picked up the kettle and filled it with water.

"Who's for coffee, and who's for tea?" Sarah asked as she went to take the kettle from Olive.

"You sit down; you need the rest," Olive said, as if it was an order.

The entire time they were in the kitchen, the twins were being passed around from one to another. "There is no doubt that they will be spoilt. Have you thought about godparents?" Angie asked.

"Last night in the hospital, John and I wrote down who we thought we would ask, and when we turned the paper over, we had both written down the same name," Sarah said excitedly.

"Go on, tell us then," Angie said, as she cuddled baby Fred.

"I can't; we haven't asked the individuals concerned yet."

"Well, that doesn't matter; we can all keep a secret," Angie replied.

"Well I suppose it wouldn't hurt as most of you are here anyway." Sarah turned to Olive. "We would like you to be godmother to Angel, along with you, Julie." She then turned to Angie. "We would like you to be godmother to Fred, and would like you to be his god-mum as well?" she said to Julie.

She then turned to Cart. "We would like you and big Fred to be godfather to Angel, and Andrew and Fred to be godfather to little Fred."

"I think we would all be honoured to accept," Andrew replied, the echo of agreement going around the kitchen.

It wasn't long before everyone had left, and John and Sarah were alone in the kitchen. Both the babies had been put down for a sleep after all the excitement of everyone taking turns of cuddling them all afternoon. Sarah sat down at the kitchen table and suddenly she burst into tears.

"What is it?" John asked, as he came to sit beside her and put his arm around her.

"I thought I was going to die. As soon as I saw Rupert, I thought I would lose my baby," Sarah said, wiping the tears from her eyes.

"You're safe now, and this time he will be locked up for good," John said.

"I know, but if Julie hadn't been there, I would have died; she was so strong. Where she got the strength to build that fire, I'll never know," Sarah said, wiping the tears from her eyes.

"She surely is remarkable," John replied, as he took the hanky out of Sarah's hand and wiped the tears from her cheek.

"Do you know that she never seemed frightened? It was as if she knew we would come out alive. I can't explain it, but I believe God spoke to her and told her we would be all right."

"You might be right; if I was God, I think I would choose her to speak to," John said with a smile.

"You're making fun of me now, but I don't care. I know what I think, and I want to do something special for her, but I don't know what," Sarah said. She pushed the chair back and stood up.

"I'm not making fun of you. I do think she is remarkable, and I'm so glad of what she did to save you. I was so afraid I had lost you, and I just wouldn't have been able to have gone on living without you." John's eyes started to fill up.

"My darling, I never thought how you would be feeling; it must have been horrendous for you." Sarah put her arms around him and hugged him tightly.

"Why don't we have a word with Olive and Angie and arrange something for Julie - perhaps a party our something?"

"I think that's a good idea," Sarah said, as she gave John a big sloppy kiss.

That afternoon, a police officer from London arrived at the Tavistock police station with Rupert Trelivan in handcuffs. "I brought you a prisoner," the officer said as he entered the station.

"It's a pity you weren't sentenced to hang last time you were in court," the Sergeant said to Rupert.

"Yeah, you would like that wouldn't you, like the rest of the peasants around here," Rupert replied in his cocky way.

"Even when you were let out, you couldn't just go," the Sergeant said.

"I don't know what you are talking about; I suggest you phone my solicitor before you ask me anything else," Rupert replied.

"I will do that right now because, trust me, I will do everything by the book. You will never ever walk away from jail again," the Sergeant said as he picked up the phone.

"How do you know his number?" Rupert asked.

"Because I phoned him this morning when I knew you were on the train; I told him what was happening."

The solicitor answered and said he would be at the station in half an hour.

"You think you're so smart," Rupert said, as the Sergeant put the phone down.

The Sergeant called a constable in. "Take Mr Trelivan down to the cells, and bring Brian Furze up to me," he said.

"What's he doing here?" Rupert asked, looking somewhat surprised.

"He is helping us with our inquiries, like you. Only he is being a bit more helpful than you."

"I knew he would not be able to keep his big trap shut!" Rupert said, as the constable led him away.

The constable soon returned with Brian Furze and took him into the interview room.

"I just want you to know that we have arrested Rupert, and he is here in a cell," the Sergeant said as he sat down in front of Furze.

"What's going to happen? You can't charge both of us," Furze said with a grin.

"Can't I? Why not - you are as much to blame as he is," the Sergeant replied.

"I didn't lock them away," Furze replied, the smile now gone from his face.

"I thought you didn't know anything about it yesterday?" The Sergeant paused and rubbed his chin. He then continued, "There is no doubt whatsoever that Rupert was responsible for locking them away, and we know you stole the key to the mine from the big house. We also know that you were in Exeter when Rupert caught the train. We also know that you visited him in prison, so I think that would be enough for any jury, so unless you got anything else to say, I think the charge against you will be aiding and abetting murder."

"I thought no one died?" Furze replied.

"That's right, but the intention was to leave them to die."

"What if I didn't know what Rupert was going to do? What if I thought he wanted the key because he had something hid there," Furze said, the smile returning to his face.

"Sounds feasible, except that you also provided him with a gun, so I think the jury will believe you knew what was going on," the Sergeant said quite calmly.

"I didn't know there were children, and that's true. I would never have gone along with it had I known." Furze was now beginning to think he had no way out.

"I do believe you. I'll tell you what I will do if you admit to what you have done and how you drove Rupert to Exeter. I can't promise, but I will have a word and see if I can just get the charge changed to supplying a firearm," the Sergeant said in a mellow tone.

"Why would you do that - you know what happened," Furze replied.

"I know, but it would save me a lot of work if you told me in a statement."

"I will make a statement, but not because of what you say. I can't help thinking about those babies," Furze replied.

The Sergeant took out a pen and a statement paper. He called over the constable to take down the statement as he went out to meet Rupert's solicitor.

The interview with Rupert and his solicitor was quite straightforward. The solicitor told Rupert that with all the evidence - and the fact that he never tried to hide his identity from Sarah and Julie - there was little point in him denying what had happened. It might have been better if he had said he just wanted to frighten them rather than kill them.

But Rupert would have none of the last bit. All he would say is, "I wish the bitches had died."

It didn't take long for the Sergeant to wrap up the interview and charge Rupert with attempted murder on four counts.

Both Rupert and Furze appeared before magistrates the following morning, and both were remanded, Rupert to Dartmoor, and Furze to Newton Abbot.

Chapter Twenty Eight

<hr>

Back at the farm, Sarah and John had returned from a day's shopping with a whole lot of baby clothes, a twin pram, another cot and a carrycot. They hadn't been home long before Sarah had the twins in the pram and pushed them down to see Julie. "What do you think?" she asked, showing off her pram.

"Very good, can I have a turn?" Julie asked with a large grin.

"You can push them up to Olive's if you like. I better show her - she was a bit concerned that I didn't have a pram for two," Sarah replied.

The pair of them made their way over to Olive's. Although Julie was pushing, Sarah had a reassuring hand on the handle. "What's up - don't you trust me?" Julie said with a bit of a giggle.

"What a question to ask after what you have done! There is no one I would trust more," Sarah said. Julie knew she meant it.

They soon got to Olive's. Angie saw them arrive, and she and Amy soon came running over.

It wasn't long before Amy was pulling back the blankets to have a look at the twins. "Can I take one out?" she asked.

"Oh no darling," Angie said. "You must leave them alone."

"It's not fair. I haven't seen them yet," Amy said with a big sulk on her face.

"If they don't wake up now, you can come over tomorrow and you can hold them if you like," Sarah said.

"That's good; I can look after them for you if you like," Amy said, now with a smile on her face.

"That will be good. I need someone to help me." Sarah put her arm around Amy and gave her a cuddle.

"Well, what else have you bought?" Olive asked.

Sarah excitedly told them everything she had bought over a cup of tea.

When they had finished their tea, Julie took the cups into the kitchen, and Sarah took the opportunity to tell Angie and Olive that she wanted to have a surprise party for Julie to thank her for saving her life.

"Angie and I will come over in the morning, and we can talk about it then," Olive whispered, as Julie returned from the kitchen.

Julie had no idea what Sarah had spoken to Angie and Olive about as Sarah and Julie made their way home.

The next morning, Angie was getting Amy her breakfast. Like every morning, Amy went out and looked over the wall to speak to Cart and Jan and watch them feed the pigs and chickens.

"Amy, breakfast!" Angie shouted, as Andrew walked in the door after his usual early morning visit to the church.

"She's not outside," Andrew said with some concern.

"Oh God, where has she gone?" Angie ran out and shouted over the wall to Cart.

Cart said, "She hasn't been here this morning. I just said to Jan that we should have waited to feed the pigs."

The phone rang, and Andrew answered it. "Have you lost something?" a voice said.

"Would it by any chance be a little girl?" Andrew answered.

"It sure is," came the reply. "She has come to help me with the twins, she tells me."

"I better shout to Angie; she's worried sick," Andrew said.

"Tell her not to worry; she's all right with me. Tell her I'll see her later."

Andrew rushed outside to Angie and told her where she was. Cart laughed. "It looks like me and you will have to take second place now Jan," he said.

Angie grabbed her coat and rushed over to the farm. "I'll give the little madam what for," she muttered under her breath, as she opened Sarah's back door. But her face lit up when she entered the kitchen, for there sitting back in the armchair was Amy, with one of the twins in her arms, feeding it a bottle.

"Hi there," Sarah said with a smile. "I've told her she can come any time, but she has to tell you where she is going."

"Thanks for that. I was worried stiff," Angie replied. "What about your breakfast, little Miss Amy?" asked Angie.

"Oh, I'm too busy at the moment," she replied, which made Angie and Sarah smile.

"Whilst you are here, can we discuss Julie's party? I'll just give Olive a ring," Sarah said as she passed the other twin to Angie.

"Mummy, do you think we could have twins?" Amy asked.

"I think Andrew might have something to say about that," Angie replied.

"I know he would say yes if I asked him," Amy said.

"Yes dear, he probably would," Angie replied with a smile.

"Olive's on her way," Sarah said. "Do you want to put a bit of toast on or something for Amy?"

Sarah had just put both the twins in the pram when Olive arrived. "I gave Fred his bottle," Amy shouted excitedly.

"Did you dear," Olive said, as she went over and kissed her on the head.

"What about this party then?" Angie said, as she put a plate of toast in front of Amy.

"Well, it has to be something special," Sarah said, her eyes filling up with a tear.

"This really means something to you, doesn't it?" Olive said as she put her arm around her.

"You will never know how much," Sarah replied. "I don't want to go into it now, but trust me, she is some special lady."

They spent the morning discussing the party. It was decided that they would ask Ben the landlord if they could hold it down at the pub, and they also decided to have a cake made. Olive had just put her notebook in her bag, when Julie appeared. "What's going on here then, having coffee without me?" she said with a smile.

Angie told her how Amy had come over, and that's how they came to be there. It wasn't long before George and Jenny appeared. "Can we take the twins for a walk?" George asked.

"Oh, I'm not sure that would be a good idea," Sarah said. "I don't think they are quite old enough for you and Jenny to take them on their own yet."

"Spoilsport," George replied.

"How about we all go?" Julie said. "It's a nice day; I'm sure we should all make the most of it."

"I think that's a good idea," Amy said, as she got down from the table and ran over to the pram.

"I'm up for that," Sarah said.

"Can me and Jenny push the pram?" George asked.

"We can take turns," Amy said, with a little voice of authority.

"You all go on. I have things to do," Olive said, as they all left the farmhouse and walked up the lane.

Olive went down to the pub to see Ben. Sarah had said that she wanted to arrange the party as soon as possible. Ben said he would do whatever they wanted, and a date was set for Saturday week.

The party was harder than expected to keep from Julie because she was always there with them all, so on the Saturday of the party, Andrew asked Julie if she would go with him to visit a parishioner over at the next village. "She is very old and feeling really down," he said, trying to convince Julie that she was needed.

Julie agreed, although thinking it strange since Andrew had never asked her to do anything like this before.

Although visiting Andrew's parishioner was used as an excuse to get Julie out of the way, Andrew did genuinely want Julie to meet this lady. He explained to Julie how he was afraid that the lady was so down that she might take her own life.

It soon became apparent how dire the situation was when they got to the old lady's house, which was extremely isolated. After a few minutes chatting with her, they learned that she had no family and no friends or neighbours.

She came across as rather charming to Julie. "You see dear," the woman said, "I have lived here my entire life; when my mother and father died, it was just me and my sister. We kept some pigs and chickens and a few sheep, and we were happy. We never wanted any men, you know," she said with a little bit of a smile.

"I think we could all do without them sometimes," Julie replied with a smile, as she caught hold of the lady's hand.

"I had to sell all our animals last week. Now that Sissy has passed away, I've got nothing now, nothing to live for."

"You must not think like that; you've got me. I'll come and see you as often as I can. Better than that, why don't you come over for dinner tomorrow. Then who knows, you might feel a lot better."

"Oh I don't know, I haven't been away from here since I left school nearly seventy years ago."

"All the more reason you should come. I tell you what - I will get my Fred to come over tomorrow morning to pick you up. If you come, we shall be delighted, but if you don't want to, that's fine."

"You seem such a dear. I will see," the old lady replied.

Andrew and Julie left and made their way back. "I'm glad you came," Andrew said. "Do you think she will come over tomorrow?"

"I know she will; I'll make sure of that. Once she gets away from there, I'm sure we can make her life worth living," Julie said.

"Do you know," Andrew said, "there are times when I could just kiss you."

"Hey, you hadn't better let Angie here you say that."

Andrew spluttered, "No - no - in a platonic way I mean." His face turned bright red.

Julie leaned over and kissed him on the cheek. "I know," she said with a smile.

They were soon back, and Andrew drove Julie right down to the lodge, just in case she saw something she shouldn't.

He needn't have worried, as everything was under control. Sarah and Olive had just taken the cake down to the pub. "Do you want me to stay home and look after the twins?" Olive asked.

"No way, they are coming with us; they've got a big thank you to say," Sarah said.

About six o'clock, Fred said, "It's been a hard day; I think we should go for a drink."

"Do you really want to? I thought we could have a quiet night in," Julie said, as she flopped down in an armchair.

This had hampered the plan. "Whatever you like - I just thought it would be nice to go out on our own for an hour."

"You've changed your tune; you never want to go out on our own," Julie said, looking surprised.

"I know, it's just because of all you have been through. I was so afraid I had lost you. I just want to sit down, the two of us, and enjoy a quiet drink and enjoy each other instead of everyone else being there."

Julie stood up and put her arms around him. "You poor dear, I don't think about you enough. I think I take you for granted sometimes, but I do love you to bits, you're still my Freddie kindness. Let me go and have a bath then. We can walk down to the pub." She leaned back and gave him a kiss. "By the way, we have a guest for dinner tomorrow," she shouted as she left the room.

Julie had her bath. She put on her jeans and red spotted top which was tied in the front, showing a little bit of midriff. She knew Fred loved this, and she was determined she would make Fred happy on their return from the pub.

"Where's Jenny?" Julie asked, as she came downstairs.

"Oh she is up with George. She is staying up there for the evening. Sarah thought it would do George good, with the twins and everything," Fred said.

These were the lines he had rehearsed a thousand times.

They left the lodge arm in arm. Making their way to the pub, Julie told Fred all about the women she had seen that day.

"It sounds like she has made a big impression on you," Fred said as he opened the pub door. Although the pub had an open floor plan, the large sitting area was approached through a large archway, which was closed off by a blanket.

"What's on?" Julie asked. "No table to sit at?"

"I got the decorators in; they promised they would finish today, but you know decorators," Ben said, as he pulled Fred's pint.

"Oh well, we will just have to sit up to the bar," Julie said with a smile.

Suddenly, the blanket covering the arch dropped to the ground, and *For She's a Jolly Good Fellow* started ringing out around the pub.

"Who are they singing to?" Julie asked, as she started to turn around. Sarah put her hand on her shoulder. "What's going on?" Julie asked, a little startled.

"It's just a little party from me to you to say thank you," Sarah said with a tear in her eye.

"Thank me? Thank me for what?" Julie replied, looking rather bemused.

"That's typical of you, you really don't know, do you? Well, let me tell you - I'm going to make a speech in a minute, and then you will know," Sarah said as she gave her a hug.

Julie turned to Fred. "Why didn't you tell me? I would have worn something different."

"You look lovely as you are," he replied. In the background, Thistle and the Cornflowers started to sing, and the entire village started to come around Julie.

"I wish I knew what this was all about," Julie said, still rather bemused.

People were mingling with one another, and the evening

was going well. The twins were sleeping even though the noise was deafening at times.

Sarah tapped hard on a glass with a spoon and shouted for quiet. "I would like you all to help yourselves to some food," she said, pointing to two long tables that had just been uncovered to expose a mountain of pasties, sandwiches, sausage rolls and much more. "Firstly though, I need to say a few words about why we are here." Sarah paused and took a long drink, and then she began.

"Just over two weeks ago, I thought I was going to die. At the time, I had no idea I was having twins. I thought I was going to lose my baby, but fortunately I had an angel with me. I cannot stress to you all what she did. She showed no fear, and she genuinely had no thought for herself. Her sole concern was for me and my baby, or babies, as it turned out. That's another story. She handled that situation as if it was something she had done a thousand times. It was cold and damp where we were, but what did my angel do? She removed her clothes and tore them into robes for my babies.

"I could see no way out, and I still believed we were doomed to die. But not Julie - she went farther into the mine, where there was a lot of dry wood. She piled it up under the tall chimney. How she did it, I will never know. Some of the pieces were three times her size. I could go on all night and never finish telling you what she did. The point of this is for me to say a big thank you to her, so Julie, will you please come up here with me, so I can thank you in front of all these people - and ask them to raise their glasses in a toast - to Julie my Angel."

Everyone raised their glasses, and *Julie* echoed around the room.

"I'm quite overwhelmed. I don't believe I did anything more than anyone else would have done. Oh, and just for the record, I was bloody scared stiff!" Julie said. She then turned and gave Sarah a big hug.

With that, the pub door opened, and in came PC Roberts. "I looked in because the village seems deserted," he said.

"That's because they are all in here," Ben the landlord replied.

The PC suddenly became very aggressive. "Whose children are these?" he asked, pointing at Amy and Spud's children. He then turned and noticed the pram. "And babies as well," he said.

"You know whose they are," Ben said rather forcefully.

"Well, this is going to have to be reported; it as an offence under the licence act to have people under the age of fourteen in a place where alcohol is sold."

"What are you going on about, you stupid bloody oaf! Go out and get on your bike," Cart said angrily.

With that, Sergeant Gibbs entered the pub. "What are you doing?" he asked the PC.

"I am just about to charge the landlord for having underage children on the premises," the PC replied.

"What!" the Sergeant exclaimed.

The PC started to stammer. "I - I - "

"Never mind - bloody well go and get on your bike, and I'll see you in the morning," the Sergeant said angrily.

The PC left with his tail between his legs.

"Would you like a drink?" Ben asked the Sergeant.

"I think a whisky would go down well, but I must have a word with Sarah a minute," he replied.

Sarah came over when she heard her name mentioned.

"I think we should just go over there where it's a bit quiet for a minute," he said, pointing to an empty table in the corner.

John, Fred and Julie went over with them. They sat down around the table. "What is it?" Sarah asked again. "Is it serious?"

"Yes," the Sergeant replied. He paused. After a little cough, he continued. "You know Rupert was sent to Dartmoor on remand?"

"Yes," Sarah said, butting in. "Don't tell me he is out."

"No, he will never be. I'm afraid he is dead."

"Dead? How do you mean dead?" John asked, with a frown.

"What I say. It appears he had a bit of a hard time of it when he was in there doing his sentence by one of the lifers; the morning he left, he apparently put something in the lifer's breakfast. Well, at dinner today, this was the first time the pair had come face to face, and the man serving life punched him. He fell over a rail on the third landing, the safety net gave way, and he fell some thirty feet and died. That's all I know at the moment."

"God, I don't know what to say, I feel quite numb," Sarah said. "I don't know if I should be glad or sad."

"Well," Julie said, "I know we should never rejoice when

someone dies, but I think it's quite all right to rejoice that he will be out of your life forever."

The Sergeant drank his whisky and left.

Once the Sergeant had gone, the people started to drift away.

John got Andrew, Angie, Cart, Olive, Fred, Julie and Sarah together.

"I think we should have a drink, and rightly or wrongly, we should thank God that Rupert is out of our lives forever."

"I'll second that," Andrew said.

"I think we can live our lives in peace now," Julie said, as she put her arm around Sarah.

Sarah gave a big sigh, and her face lit up. "I know now that me and my babies will be safe for ever."